"SILHOUETTE"

REFLECTIONS of A

CHRISTIAN STRIPPER

By: Felicia Lowery Fewell

Silhouette Reflections of a Christian Stripper

ISBN: 978-0-9963097-0-7

First Printing July 2015

Printed in the United States of America

For information write to:

Fewell Publishing Company

P.O. Box 1573

Waldorf, Md. 20604

Email: fewellfelicia@gmail.com

Cover design by: Felicia Kierra (feliciadew@hotmail.com)

Introduction

Born the daughter to a preacher and his wife, my name is Lorraine. I have a life of the not so typical preacher's kid or PK as most people in the Christian sector refer to us. I attend an all-girl private school where I'm an Honor Roll student. My world consist only of school, church, prayer, and fasting, and more school, church, prayer and fasting. Never allowed to wear pants, only dresses or skirts down past my knees and blouses up to my chin. The only television we are allowed to watch is Christian programming. Gospel and classical are the only genres of music that we listen to. Classically trained, I sing and play several instruments, but my favorites are the Violin and Piano. Most people say I do quite well as the leader of the Youth Music Ministry at my dad's church. The shy one, and middle child of three girls; my older sister's name is Lena, we are 16 months apart, and LeAnn is the baby of the family. My only friends are my sisters, kids at my daddy's church and a few at my school. However, I spent most of my free time with my very popular best friend Kia. Her strong presence seemed to create a shield that makes it okay for me to be awkward yet accepted by some. I'm definitely not in the popular club. I am tall, gangly, and four-eyed with braces that attempt to straighten my very crooked teeth. Mocha colored skin and hair down to the middle of my back. But, mom keeps our hair wrapped up into a very tight bun because my dad believes that only married women should wear their hair down. I consider myself a good girl who follows all of the rules set by my parents and the adults around me. Dad and mom are very strict and protective over us, but tragedy has caused me to slip away from their vice grip. I've decided to trade in my violin and piano skills to dance for dollars. The Lorraine inside of me has died. My new name is Silhouette, and you can find me on a pole or stage giving a lap dance at a strip club near you.

The life of a preacher's kid can sometimes be a hard pill to swallow. Unlike normal children there is an astronomical amount of pressure that comes along with that birthright. You're not allowed to make the same mistakes as your peers. PK's mistakes are always a direct reflection of our almost perfect parents, and you are judged more harshly than others. My daddy is the Founder and Senior Pastor of two local churches one on the North side the other on the South side of town. Both his congregations are large, and membership is steady growing. To me and my sisters he's just our daddy, Kirk Logan the protector of our lives and home. My father is really intelligent. He attended a Division 1 College where he played the Center position on their basketball team on a full scholarship. He is a tall, robust guy and takes education very seriously. Dad double majored in both Political Science, and Theology all while minoring in Business, and he still managed to graduate Summa Cum Laude. He has sat amongst some of the most prominent leaders in the city while serving on countless committees to assist in governing legislative affairs. So to the people in church and the community he is Pastor Logan a well-known and respected leader in the city. He does a lot of outreach in the community; visiting the sick, feeding the hungry and homeless. My father also provides new clothes,

3

shoes, and school supplies for children in low-income families. We live a pretty decent lifestyle, residing in a middle class mixed neighborhood. Our home is very nice, and would show like a model. The area is filled with manicured lawns and neatly trimmed trees. My family has three cars, and we take two vacations every year. But the most amazing trip for me was our visit to Jerusalem with the church last summer. Everyone was baptized in The Jordan River where it is said that Jesus was baptized by John the Baptist. Wherever my family traveled we were always together. I had an undying love for God and the ministry, and I'd hoped to someday follow my daddy's footsteps.

My mom Camille is a really attractive woman, docile, and very attentive to her family especially my dad. One of mommy's rules are unless my dad wasn't at the dinner table we are not allowed to touch our food until he takes his first bite, she says it's out of respect because he was the head of our family. But she's the perfect First Lady of the church, and I admire her. You could tell that mom has some diversity in her gene pool. But, sadly, she doesn't know her true nationality nor identity. She was adopted when she was 3 months old after being left abandoned in a box next to a trash can in an alley. Her skin tone is mocha like mine and she has big hazel brown eyes with dark features, which are really exotic in nature. Like all of her girls her hair flows down her back except she wears hers that way. There were countless times when we were out in public places, and Native Ethiopians spoke to her in their Amharic tongue. Mommy always looked absolutely puzzled because she didn't understand the Semitic language that they were speaking. Although she did bear a striking resemblance the mystery of her true nationality has yet to unfold. My daddy provided a good life for us. But he spent a lot of time away from home, busy serving the people at the church and in the community. He traveled extensively speaking at Political and Religious conferences and church banquets. It seemed the only time we really saw him was in the pulpit, at the dinner table when he wasn't traveling, on vacations, or when he was whipping my oldest sister for some form of repeated misbehavior. Otherwise he was tucked away in one of his three offices working on sermons or some type of political affair.

Daddy was indeed the disciplinary, and I understood clearly the consequences if we were disobedient to our parents. My older sister Lena seemed to buck against the rules often. I witnessed the many punishments that ranged from memorizing and reciting scriptures, to kneeling for long periods of time while balancing really heavy books in the palms of our hands with your arms extended outward. However, when you made the mistake of dropping the book, and believe me it was an inevitable occurrence, or not reciting the scriptures verbatim, you would be whipped with an extension cord. After enduring years of what she called senseless acts of cruelty, Lena refused the punishments and went straight for the beatings instead. When she was 16, against mother's wishes she walked out of the house with her hair down, but when she returned dad shaved her head completely bald as a form of punishment. She cried out of sheer anger and humiliation. I felt so bad for her and she had to go to school wearing head wraps until her hair grew back. I asked, Lena why don't you just listen to them and avoid the trouble? With the look of disgust she replied, I hate that man, and momma is stupid for staying with him, as soon as I turn 18 I'm leaving. After that conversation with my sister, I did notice that dad treated momma more like his child rather than a wife. But it had always been that way, so it was normal behavior in my eyes. However, something was definitely happening with Lena but I couldn't understand it, all I knew was she didn't get along with neither of our parents under any circumstances.

My best friend Kia's parents Greg and Rebecca have been friends with my parents ever since I can remember; they are also members of my daddy's church. Kia and I have attended the same schools since 1st grade. But, her parents aren't as strict as mine; our fathers are childhood friends, and her dad is a deacon at our church. However, Deacon Greg allowed Kia to wear tight jeans and all of the latest fashions along with the hair styles that were trending. It was the good old 80's, and we were entering our first year of high school in the upcoming fall. Still a private school except it was co-ed. The excitement of having my braces removed over the summer had set in, and I was ready to show off my new smile. But, being around boys made me nervous. The only boys that I'd ever been around were either cousins or boys in my Sunday school classes. Not to mention that most of them picked on me anyway, I was considered the weird nerdy church girl. Go-go music was hot and originated in my home city of Washington, DC during the mid-1960's to the late 1970's. It has a real upbeat tempo with drums, horns, bongos, timbales, cowbells and features some of DC's greatest musical artist. This music is sort of a subgenre, it combines "Funk, Rhythm & Blues, and Hip Hop" that is sure to make anyone dance, and is still very popular today. But, these genres were emerging into a new age form of Hip Hop and Rap music that were on the rise. This new style of music was hot and spreading like wild fire. Kia let me listen to it during my weekend visits, and I really enjoyed secular music. Go-go and Rap music was nothing like the gospel or classical that I was forced to listen to, it made me want to dance. But guilt rode my back for listening to it, let alone liking it. I often prayed to ask God for forgiveness for my dishonesty, and the thought of confessing to my parents that I'd listened to secular music crossed my mind several times. However, they would cut off my friendship with Kia and I didn't want that, so as quickly as the thought came, it left my mind. Kia and I had totally opposite personalities, she was funny and I was dry, she was popular and I wasn't. We both were avid readers, but while I was reading Christian based literature she was reading steamy hot novels that would have burned the very soul from your body.

My first year of high school was stressful, I was tackling all AP courses, but making straight A's. I'd become very active academically, as the President of the Student

Government and the student council. I sang with the school chorus and had been inducted into The National Honor Society. I was also an honorary member of the chess club all while hitting the books hard. Kia was doing all of the fun things that I wasn't allowed to do like cheerleading, school dances, and going to parties, she even had a boyfriend.

When I asked my parents about doing things like joining the cheerleading team, going to school dances that I'd helped organize as President of The Student Council; or even wearing shorts for gym without wearing a dress to cover them the answer was always no. Frustrated, because I didn't understand why I couldn't do things that normal teenagers were doing. My parent's thoughts were that tight clothing would only draw negative attention. Then they reminded me that we had a reputation to uphold as Christian people. I guess PK really stands for "PERFECT KID", so I made every attempt to let go of my ideas but I had zero understanding of what the big deal was. My sophomore year was worse than my freshman year. It seemed that my parents and I were clashing more than ever. I continued to follow the rules as I was told, but every now and then I'd respectfully ask for some leniency. My parents felt that my continuous questionings were disrespectful; all

I wanted to do was fit in with kids my age. But the law in my house has always been, do what you're told and never question parental authority.

There was a cute boy in my Chemistry class named Vincent, a Math and Sciences geek, and my partner on an upcoming science project. He's really tall for a high school kid, a pretty boy, with curly hair, big green eyes that changed colors, and the deepest dimples I'd ever seen, they were even deeper than my baby sister LeAnn's. Vincent was the only boy that ever said anything nice to me, which was real cool, and I did like him. He became my new topic of conversation whenever Kia and I were together. His personality was sweet and we talked quite a bit in class while working on our project; and he'd walk the halls with me and Kia between classes sometimes. I didn't think too much about why he was so nice until he put his phone number in my hand. I looked at it but I was not allowed to talk to boys on the phone so I attempted to give it back. Kia of course knew the real deal about my obvious crush, but she also knew how strict my parents were. She sucked her teeth, snatched the number out of my hand and said "Girl I'll hold it for you". But, what Vincent or Kia didn't know is that phone number was commemorated to memory at first glance. We began talking on the phone at Kia's house every chance I got. She had her own phone line in her bedroom, talk about privileged. If I wasn't talking on the phone with my grand-parents, I wasn't talking on the phone at all in my house. Well, maybe to Kia for no more than the10 minute timespan twice a week that my dad allotted for only her.

Kia and I shared everything, we were like sisters with no secrets. She told me about her first time having sex with her boyfriend Andre, and how they do it every time they see each other, except when she's on her period. I was amazed; and she gave me all the juicy details from start to finish. The stories made me blush with embarrassment yet, they left me intrigued with curiosity. This girl is crazy cool and the funniest person that I know. Our parents are very close friends and she had everybody fooled. My father often referred to her as his own daughter because he thought she was a perfect little angel. All the adults boast of her being a well-mannered child, when really she's a wild child in disguise. It was so funny but her good girl act was a part of the reason that my parents never had a problem with me spending time away from home with her and her family.

The summertime was quickly approaching, and we would be spending the entire break together between my house, and at hers. My parents made it clear that just because I was on break from school, and Kia's parents allowed her to stay home from church some days does not mean that I could do the same. As long as I came to Bible study, Sunday service, and choir rehearsal I could spend the summer break with my girl. During one of my visits with Kia, a girl named Eva from our school was having a party, she insisted that we both go. I replied, Girl, you know better than that, and if my parents found out they would kill me. Kia's mom was cool with me going but told me that I had to call my parents to get permission, and I knew that was out of the question. Old clever Kia, before I could get out a word she lied to her mom saying, she already called and her dad said it was okay. Afraid, I said "Girl what if my father finds out" Gritting her teeth she says "he won't". No Kia! I'm going to stay here, you go ahead, then you could tell me about it when you get back. Then she says "Girl, you're going because guess what" What? Vincent is going to be there. Gasping for air I replied ARE YOU SERIOUS? My heart sank into my feet, I had to go. This was my only chance to be around him outside of school. But, on the other hand, what if my folks find out? I was wrestling with the Demon of Decision and Satan clearly won that round because against everything that's right in my world I decided to go anyway. Kia looked so fly in her designer jeans, and fresh kicks rocking her Asymmetric hair style. I went into Kia's en suite to change because that's the rule in my house. No one outside of my mother has ever seen me undressed, not even my own sisters. I put on my best dress feeling good, thinking it was the bomb, but when I emerged from the bathroom Kia laughed me out saying, WHERE IN THE HELL DO YOU THINK YOU'RE GOING WITH THAT UGLY ASS DRESS ON? YOU AIN'T WEARING THAT SHIT! My jaw dropped and I asked, well what am I supposed to wear then? I attempted to pull out another dress but she forcefully smacked it out of my hand yelling, IF YOU DON'T GET THAT SHIT OUT OF HERE! Then Kia snatched my bag from me and hurled it across the room. With my head tipped slightly to the right side, eyes wide open and the expression of surprise on my face, we both laughed so hard. Her mouth is so trashy but, she is too funny. We were about the same size so Kia went into her closet and pulled out a pair of jeans, a shirt and some sneakers. I'd never worn a pair of jeans in my life and was really nervous about it. I turned to go back into her personal bathroom when she yells WHERE YOU GOING? To change I replied! Sucking her teeth and rolling her eyes she says "Girl we got the same damn thing why you hiding? To shut her mouth I slipped the jeans on while still wearing the dress and quickly pulled the dress over my head trying to cover myself while attempting to put on the shirt. Surprisingly the jeans although tight were quite comfortable. The look on Kia's face made me wonder if she had seen a ghost.

When I looked in the mirror hanging on the back of her bedroom door I discovered my very curvaceous figure. Kia said OH MY GOD GIRL, YOU GOT A BUMPIN ASS SHAPE! That was DC lingo for describing something good. Still wearing the tight bun she suggested I take my hair down so she could curl it; then she gave me some lip gloss to complete my new look. Shocked at the drastic makeover my self-esteem shifted upward just a little. I felt different and to my surprise I was just as pretty as the other girls at my school. My father always reminded me that the inner appearance is more important than the outward appearance, but I sure felt pretty outside.

Kia and I finally arrived at the house party being held in the basement of Eva's house. Most of the people there were students from my school everybody was staring but nobody recognized me right away. Not wearing my glasses and squinting to see, spotting Vincent was easy. I made my way over, tapped him on his shoulder I said "Hello". He replied "How are you"? I'm fine. Then he did a double take, Lorraine! Girl you look different! In a timid voice my response was, I know. He said this is the first time I ever seen you in pants, and I replied me too because this is the first time I've ever worn them. We laughed then Vincent took my hand and said you should wear pants more often, which made me blush as we stood in the corner talking. Kia and some of the popular girls came over and rudely pulled me away. They were ranting and raving about how different I looked. But, they weren't the only ones who noticed, so did all of the boys that wouldn't give me the time of day until now. Almost every boy there asked me to dance, but I declined every invitation. Outside of a little church shout I wasn't much of a dancer anyway; and besides the only boy that had my interest was Vincent. I went back to the corner where he waited for me, to continue our conversation.

The music was really loud. Everybody was doing the latest dances like the Happy Feet, Roger Rabbit, and The Cabbage Patch. The DJ played some Rap music and some of the boys started Break Dancing. Vincent got on the floor where they were battling, and it was obvious that nobody could beat him, this boy moves were tight. My eyes were filled with stars just watching him, and when the battle was over he came back to talk to me. A slow song came on and somebody turned off the lights. He asked if I wanted to dance. I divulged my secret that I didn't know how. He grabbed my hand and pulled me close, my body was stiff as a board, then he whispered in my ear relax and let me lead you. My palms were getting sweaty but I did my best to go along. He said you're not a bad dancer. I smiled and said no you're just a good teacher. Then out of nowhere the thought of what my father would do to me if he walked in right now almost made me sick to my stomach. So I stopped him. What's wrong Lorraine? I'm thirsty. He got me some punch and we spent the rest of the night just talking and holding hands occasionally. This party was the most fun I'd had so far. When we got back to Kia's I called him almost immediately trying not to seem too anxious but, I was. The conversation lasted until we both fell asleep still holding the phone. We went to a few more parties that summer, the more I went, the more relaxed I became in the atmosphere. That summer changed my life, it taught me that there was a life filled with excitement outside of my parent's protective bubble. Wearing Kia's jeans became the norm; I loved my new weekend look and so did my new friends.

However, fall came quickly and school started again, I'd return to my nerdy look with the tight hair bun and the corky glasses. It was my junior year and my oldest sister Lena had left home for good. We barely saw much of her, daddy didn't allow her in the house because she'd left against his wishes. I was not allowed to ask any questions or even discuss the matter with my parents. Lena really didn't have a steady place to stay but when nobody was home I would sneak her in so she could shower and eat. Sometimes I'd let her sleep in my room on the floor but, on the opposite side of my bed just in case one of my parents came in they wouldn't see her. The thought of my sister not having any place to lay her head while she was on the streets weighed heavily on my heart and mind, and I couldn't sleep many nights. I really looked up to my big sister and begged her to come back home. I'd overheard my father on several occasions say to my mom that he would allow her back if she agreed to follow the rules and go back to school. Lena dropped out of school in her senior year without anyone knowing until my parents were informed that she couldn't graduate because she had not been to school in more than 6 months. Lena refused to come back saying that the price was too high. It seemed that now I was going down the same path that she'd gone with them.

Clashing with my parents often, Lena warned me to watch myself but, I wasn't sure what she meant by that.

My 16th birthday seemed to have given birth to an even stronger interest in the male species especially Vincent. We saw each other in school and on most weekends, he'd started coming to my church sometimes. But, my parents only knew him as a schoolmate and nothing more. Things were definitely changing for me, I would leave home, change into pants at my girl Kia's house and we'd go hang out. My friends became more accepting of me now that they saw I had a cool side. I'd even developed a habit of cussing but only around them, although I'd almost slipped in front of my parents a few times when they would get on my nerves. My friends and I hung out at the arcade, the movies every once in a while, and a few other places so Vincent and me got to spend so much time together. Kia's birthday is two weeks after mine, but she had her father wrapped around her finger. He bought her a brand new car for her 16th birthday so we were rolling every chance we got. After our dates at the skating rink on Saturday nights we would all chill in the parking lot blasting the music and joking around. I was sitting on Vincent's lap, when he gently swept my hair over my left shoulder, and kissed the back of my neck so softly, for the first time something new was happening in my lower extremities. I stopped him, but really liked how it made me feel. This must be that thing Kia experienced all the time with her boyfriend Andre. What are you doing boy, as if it really mattered? He smiled and said enjoying you. Vincent is so fine, and when I looked into those green eyes that changed to blue when his mood was serious, it made me melt into a position of vulnerability. Then he commenced to lay the most passionate kiss on me that I'd never had. Both sweet and very endearing it was my first kiss; but sort of awkward for me because I didn't know what I was doing. But that kiss made it official, he asked if he could be my boyfriend, and of course I said yes. I fell deeply in love with him that night. But my parents were locked out of my secret, because this would never be acceptable behavior for any of their daughters. I knew it was wrong sneaking around to do the things that my parents would never allow me to do. However, right, wrong, or indifferent making my own choices was so freeing to my soul, and the happiest time of my life. But this was about to take a drastic turn for the worst.

On one of my weekend outings we were hanging out at the local burger spot, when in walks one of the church busy bodies. She was notorious for spreading all the latest news and gossip. Ms. Valencia saw me wearing pants with my hair flowing free, and to top it off I was wearing makeup. My boyfriend was standing with his body smashed closely against mine with his arms wrapped around my waist. In a high pitched tone of shock, Sister Valencia yelled Lorraine! I stood stuck in that spot like a deer in headlights. Immediately shock caused a couple of my natural senses to leave my body. It was like someone snatched away my vocal cords, I couldn't speak. I just stood there with my jaw dropped as everything seemed to be moving in super slow motion. Her mouth was moving but I couldn't hear her words. However, I knew she would run straight to my father and tell him everything.

Goddammit! I was absolutely right, she must've went straight to my house from the burger place, because although me and Kia immediately jumped in the car and raced back to her house, we pulled up the same time he did. Usually mommy comes to get me whenever I visit Kia, but she and my little sister were out of town so my father came to pick me up. Still in pants and a full face of makeup with my hair flowing I was caught. He didn't even give me a

chance to get my things out of her house. GET
YOURSELF IN THIS CAR! Yes sir. What was about to
happen next was a grotesque act of cruelty.

The ride home was grueling, daddy was furious to say the
least, he was screaming about how I was changing since I'd
started the co-ed high school, and that boys only want one
thing, to get in my pants. Daddy quickly reminded me with
the voice of thunder I'm raising you to be pure in the eyes
of God. He started comparing me to Lena saying, you're
not going to be a whore like she is. My mouth dropped
open because I knew it would be hell to pay. I'd never
heard my daddy say things like that before. I rode home in
complete silence, with my head hanging low, riddled with
guilt and shame. A daddy's girl but, I'd done the very thing
that he despised most, lied and caused embarrassment and
bought disgrace to God, the church, and my family. When
we got home daddy told me to strip down and he left the
room for a minute. Embarrassed that my dad was going to
see me undressed, I peeled away every layer of my clothing
slowly. His anger let me know that the punishment was
going to be harsh. This would be the very first time that I'd
ever been physically reprimanded by either of my parents.

Daddy always said I was his favorite, but he didn't give me any slack or sympathy for all of my good behavior up until this point. I was about to pay a harsh price for the only indiscretion that I'd ever committed. Undressed standing in the center of the room wearing nothing but my bra and panties. The remnants of makeup smeared across my face as I made every effort to wipe the fear away, while trying to cover my bare body all at once. But, the tears continued to fall like rain and I knew this whipping was going to be severe. However, guilt wouldn't allow me to speak a word or try to plead my case, because I knew better than to disobey my parents. Daddy walked back into the room and snatched his belt from his pants like a slave master about to crack his whip. Yelling this is what happens to fast little girls. Just when I braced myself for the first lashing the unthinkable happened, he pushed me down and pinned me to the floor. Using the weight of his large body and one hand he gripped both of my skinny wrists forcefully pressing my arms to the floorboard above my head. With his free hand he ripped away my panties, and vigorously stuck his penis inside of me. I screamed in agony because the pain was like nothing I had ever felt before. It felt like what I'd imagined the pain caused by a dull knife being forcefully pushed through the thick layers of skin before puncturing a deep hole in my heart and leaving my existence in ruins. He covered my mouth to muffle my cries. I couldn't fight back he was too strong and I was powerless against him. I was able to free my hands long enough to scratch him across his face, but he slapped me, and threatened to snap my neck if I didn't shut my mouth and stop moving. I called out to God and He obviously couldn't hear or understand me because my inarticulate cries went unanswered. In disbelief that I was being beaten, raped, and at the same time losing my virginity all at the hands of my father was too much to bear, it was like a horrible nightmare. Stuck in this surreal act of reality my mind drifted off into unchartered territory. Why is my dad hurting me, and how is it that my cries for God are void and unanswered. The man that had protected me all of my life, and up until this point was the only man that I'd ever trusted was now hurting me more than I'd ever been hurt before. He was saying some very lustful and distasteful things; telling me how good I was, and that he had been waiting to see how I felt inside. This man said I felt better than my sister because she was a whore who wasn't a virgin anyway. His actions along with his words were an obvious sign that this was a premeditated, and anticipated act on his part. I now understood why Lena hated him so much, and her warning made perfect since now. Could it be possible that mommy knew that daddy was raping my sister but, stood by and did nothing to protect her? The drops of sweat falling from his face into my eyes and mouth left a burning, disgusting salty taste. There was a distant look in his eyes that I had never seen before. Lena on the other hand had obviously been attacked by this monster numerous times before she ran away. He didn't look like himself and I was scared for my life. Mortified, my mind was in a tailspin, it didn't seem real. I only wish my sister would have told me the whole truth.

It seemed like eternity but he finally let me go, I got up slowly doubled over clinching my stomach in excruciating pain with blood and my daddy's semen running down my legs. Crying and shaking with fear, shock, pain, and disgrace I went into the bathroom and locked the door behind me. Got in the shower and turned the water on as hot as I could stand it, and slide to the shower floor to let the water run over my head hoping to die or at least drown out all the pain. Rubbing my skin almost raw trying to scrub away the stench of daddy's sexual assault. Worrying if he would do this to me again, wondering where my big sister was. I had absolutely no understanding of how this man of The Clothe who was so revered in the Christian and secular community could be such a monster inside of his own home. I didn't know how much time had gone by while sitting on the shower floor with that violent scene replaying over and over in my head. It must've been a while because I feel asleep; only to be awakened with cold water rolling over my body and a very loud pounding on the bathroom door. I could hear the roaring voice of the rapist on the other side yelling for me to come out. Afraid to speak, I quickly got out of the shower still dripping wet suffering in pain with vaginal bleeding and the sting of raw friction that he'd left between my legs. I wrapped myself in a towel, my mind was so warped that I didn't think to grab any clothing. Stuck with nowhere to run, there was no way to escape the second floor bathroom void of windows. He continued to bang on the door and threatened to break it down, trembling I shouted, I'll be out in a minute! The sound of his footsteps let me know he'd walked away, and I stood there for a few more minutes afraid to open the door. I had to eventually come out so I slowly emerged to see if he was there, it felt like a scene in one of the horror movies that I'd seen with my friends.

I rushed to my bedroom and locked the door. Put on a nightgown, and a pad to catch the blood, got in my bed and pulled the covers over my head. Laying there crying as silently as I could thinking, if daddy was so adamant about me being pure in the eyes of God, why was he the one to defile my body while God watched him do it. After about ten minutes I could hear him coming down the hallway. Petrified, and shaking with fear when he attempted to turn the door knob and tried to come in. When he discovered the door was locked he said in a very calm tone, Lorraine open the door. His tone was almost like the dad that I'd known and loved my whole life. I didn't answer right away but, he continued to knock, afraid to make him angry I opened the door. Maybe he was coming to say he was sorry, or maybe he wasn't.

He entered my room and tried to hug me, I jumped out of sheer terror at his attempt to touch me and stood in complete silence. There was a huge lump in my throat and my heart felt very heavy. He sat down on my bed but I tried to keep my distance by standing at the door. Come and have a seat next to me Lorraine. I wanted to run so badly, but that wasn't an option. When I sat down at the far end of the bed he said, you know I was just showing you what would happen to you if you don't listen to what I tell you to do. Lost and bewildered I couldn't speak, my mind was completely blown away with emotional stress. The physical trauma to my body was so painful and the blood flowed heavily, what was I supposed to say to this man.? Thinking to myself, does he really think that I'm that naive to believe that he didn't enjoy what he did to me? The look in his eyes told me that there would be more acts of violence. The one way conversation wasn't going well and my intuition was correct. This animal that mirrored my dad started fondling me again. I begged and pleaded with him to stop but, my vulnerability seemed to fuel the fire in him. He forcefully pinned me down, twisting my arms and brutally raped me again, but this time I was sodomized. The pain was unbearable, and my bed looked like someone had been murdered there. And though I was still breathing, death seemed to be in close proximity. Needless to say this went on for the remainder of the weekend. I was completely numb and mortified when mommy returned three days later. The look on her face when she came into my room to greet me told me that she knew something was wrong. I immediately broke down and told her about what he done to me, but was frantic at her response. Momma looked me straight in my eyes with tears streaming down her face and replied, there is nothing I can do. She further warned that what goes on in our house better stay in our house, because the consequences would be far worse than what I'd already encountered. My spirit, soul, and body died that day, what was I going to do?

My head space was twisted up in a tornado of thoughts that sent me into a massive panic attack. Who was this man that I'd loved and respected so much, and why did mom act as if nothing happened? What did I do to turn my father into this monster? Now I was certain that he had done the same thing to my older sister, it was clear this was the reason for her acts of rebellion. Mom's passive attitude that dismissed her husband's behavior, and her ability to pretend that she wasn't just informed that her husband was a rapist that attacks his own children leaves me puzzled. She stood by and did nothing to comfort or protect me, not a hug an apology or even an ounce of compassion and getting the necessary medical attention was out of the question. Her tears were for herself and I knew that once she warned me to keep this act of violence to myself. And if god was so real, where in the hell was he? I had to get out! But, there was nowhere for me to run. Trapped in this labyrinth of mass destruction with a rapist and his accomplice. The spirit of melancholy overwhelmed me because until now they seemed to be my loving parents. When all they really are is Bible carrying wolves in Christian clothing, using the church as their platform to prey on the weak and innocent.

Every day that I stayed in their house the tick tock of time chipped away at my existence. I'm losing more of myself and there is a deep dark space within where emptiness permeates my soul.

The world looks completely different through my eyes now. Trust, love, respect and faith in a god are all out of focus. However, fear, hate, despair and grief along with disbelief in everything and everyone seems to be in clear view. I hated the whole idea of church and the people within those walls. It was Ms. Valencia's nosey ass that delivered me to my father, the pastor that fleeced me of my innocence. The first lady posing as my mother who wasn't first at anything except compensating her husband at her daughter's expense, and god who is now the author and finisher of my doubt & unbelief. My relationship with my friends began to dwindle because I crawled back into my old shell of silence; and they never really questioned my behavior. As far as they were concerned the old Lorraine was back. My visits to Kia's house were cut off completely. Our parents had a huge blow-out that caused her family to leave the church. My father blamed them for my disobedience. Kia and I are still friends but we have very limited interactions, only between classes and at lunch period. I felt responsible for the disconnection between the two families that had been so close since my childhood. Vincent approached me apologizing for the trouble, asking me what happened, and if I were okay. I am fine, please don't feel bad about the choices that I made. He asked "Is there anything I can do"? No. Why are you so short with me Lorraine? No reason, I have a lot on my mind. I have to go Vincent and I walked away. He called out Lorraine! Lorraine! I said nothing, and kept on walking. He knew something was wrong because there was a serious wedge between us now. But I never told anyone what happened, who would believe me anyway, and I'd already been warned of the consequences so I guess I'll be taking this to my grave.

Seems the more Vincent tried to get closer to me the further away I intentionally pushed him. My life was ruined now, he knew that I was a virgin and he respected that fact. He had only one sexual encounter when he was 14, but was practicing abstinence. Our plans were to get married right after college, and he would be my first. We were going to focus on our amazing careers as a Psychiatrist and a Chemical Engineer, buy our forever home in California and have three perfect children. But, now that I had been deflowered numerous times by my own father how was I going to explain my broken hymen? The memory of

Vincent's gentle touch and our first kiss was so dear to my heart. Yet, now when he touches me my flesh crawls because all I feel is my father's attacks, and I was doing my very best not to let him see it. I did everything I could do to run him away but he refused to let me go. I knew I liked Vincent but, I was really confused about love now. I don't understand how someone could willingly and collectively gives life to a child, then turn and rip the soul of that child apart the way my parents did my sister and me. If that's love, then I don't want it, and damn sure don't need it. I am now damaged goods, tampered with and plucked away like ashes blowing in the wind, and Vincent deserves someone better than me.

In an effort to maintain what little sanity I had left, my total focus became my studies and school work. I was able to score a perfect 1600 on the SAT; and as my senior year came to a close my test scores and acceptance letters to multiple schools gave me the competitive edge I needed to leave DC, and escape this nightmare. Prom was out of the question for me, my father made that clear, and I had no desire to go anyway. I told Vincent to go with someone else, this was yet another tactic to push him away, but he continued to refuse. It was clear that he was not going anywhere so I had no other option. I did one of the hardest

31

things that I'd ever had to do "break up with my First Love". It was painful for me, and my approach was so cruel, shallow, and cold. He met me at my locker like he did every day, only this time would be really different. When he moved in to hug me I forcefully pushed him away. I started yelling and screaming at him to leave me alone. This bought a lot of attention to us and his big beautiful smile was replaced with the look of confusion. Begging and pleading "What did I do Lorraine"? Just leave me alone Vincent; and without any explanation I broke his heart. He looked in my eyes and guilt would barely allow me to look into his; the last words that he spoke to me were, "You're not mad at me, and I don't know what happened to you that night, but whatever it was it changed who you are, and it also changed us". I love you and always will Lorraine, I only want you to be happy, and he turned and walked away. I felt like the worst person in the world. The weeks leading up to graduation were awkward and very painful. He did make several more attempts to win me back. Notes, gifts, he even tried to meet me between classes to talk, but I did everything I could do to avoid him.

Graduation day was the last time I'd seen or heard from him. He and I were Salutatorian and Valedictorian and we both spoke at our graduation. I was devastated to say the least, here we were once again working together, and it was our intellect that put us both on that platform. We could have taken the world by storm but circumstances would take us in opposite directions.

This summer was different from every other summer that I have ever had. I'd changed in ways that even I didn't understand. But it was time for me to go out and see what else the world had to offer. My mind was finally made up about the college that I decided to attend far away from this horrible place. But not before my abortion that's scheduled for the upcoming week. I was lonely, depressed and now 14 weeks pregnant by my father. Not the graduation gift that I wanted or expected, but when I walked across the stage to receive my High School Diploma I wasn't walking alone. My womb housed my twin siblings that also doubled as my children. My holier than thou parents suddenly believed in an abortion to cover up their bullshit. He always preached that abortion was no different than murder in the eyes of this so called god that he served. Sickened with hatred, and disgust watching my mother as she sat in the pulpit and smile like only the first lady could; while her husband preached against fornication and adultery but his seeds were growing inside of me. "I guess rape was okay, because he was guilty of the act so he never mentioned that subject". GO FIGURE! All I wanted was those foul souls out of my body before I experienced movement that would signify that all of this was real. The day came and my mother secretly took me to the abortion clinic to pull the twin sins from my womb. With no support as usual she dropped me off at the front door, and informed me that she was going to the mall but would be back to pick me up in a few hours. When I walked inside of the dark gloomy office, fear started to overtake me. I made my way to the front desk to sign in and pay the $250.00 fee. There was an eeriness' hovering over the place, and a death-like silence in the room. The atmosphere was cold and uncomfortable. As I sat there filling out the paperwork, waiting to be called to the back, I looked at the other 4 girls who were waiting as well. I wondered what their stories were, how did they get here? Despite the "Why & How", we all had a couple of things in common; we were nothing more than numbers to the staff, and we all would be responsible for the deaths of at least 6 babies that day. They took me back but my first stop was to a small office to speak with a Counselor that looked at me like I had some sort of contagious disease. She told me that her job was to be certain that the abortion was my own choice and not the decision of someone else. She also gave me a packet loaded with information about the services available to teens in distress. Once that was over a nurse came to take me down to the room. As I followed her down the long, cold, hallway that led to an all-white box shaped room where the procedure was going to take place, the nurse started to explain the procedure. I wanted to get it over with so I hurried to sign the last of the papers giving permission to terminate the pregnancy. The nurse numbed my cervix and it was a bit uncomfortable. My mind attempted to go into fight or flight mode, but I was able to pull myself back together. When the Doctor and his assisting nurse entered the room, his callous disposition suggested that he'd been in this business for far too long. He didn't speak, he instructed me to lay back and he pushed my legs open. The painful process took less than 15 minutes. When he was done he simply stood up, removed his bloody gloves, washed his hands, and walked out of the room without uttering a word.

Although I had no emotional attachment to the babies something other than those children were snatched away from me that day. I laid in the recovery room for 2-3 hours thinking about Vincent and the look on his face when I ran him away. He was my best friend and those children should have been his like we had pre-planned for our future. Vincent and I had no secrets until that night, and the last words that he spoke to me were "I don't know what happened to you that night but it changed who you are". He was absolutely right, because rape and incest at the hands of a girl's own father will change everything. I never thought that I would be entangled in a sick twisted physical and psychological Menage a' trois with my parents; where the father physically fucks his daughters while his wife, the mother sits and watches her husband sexually assaults their babies, and does nothing except keep their nasty secret.

 The feeling of excruciating cramps and hemorrhaging from the procedure was present. I was left alone in my room from dusk until dawn to care for myself during the 4 day healing process. My mom never came once in the 4 days to check on me. During that time I only ate one meal a day if that because I was too weak to go up and down the stairs. But the physical pain could never trump the emotional distress that I constantly felt. Suicide was a daily thought in my head, and prayer would have been my alternative but, I no longer pray because I no longer believe. How could the God of all things good that I'd learned to love my entire life allow such nasty, twisted, lascivious acts of sufferings to be inflicted on innocent people? I was taught that God would never leave me, yet I was definitely abandoned by mom and both my natural and spiritual fathers. This god and his word had to be some sort of mythical illusion that clouds the minds of those who believe as I once did. I was certain that none of this could be real; if so what was it that I'd done or sown as the church teaches that was causing me to reap this type of punishment repeatedly. My father continued to rape me until the day that I left for college and like always mom never did or said anything. I think she hated me as much as I hated her.

Fall couldn't come quick enough for me. I was off to one of the most prestigious Universities in the rural part of Georgia, on a scholarship far away from my abusers. Pre-Med is my major and I have set high expectations for myself with no plans of ever going back home. My roommate Robin Coles is very nice. She was from Atlanta Georgia about 2 hours away from our school studying Pre-Law. She's a Southern Belle, beautiful girl short in stature and very sweet. I had just missed meeting her parents because I'd gotten lost on the large campus with no help from anyone. Unlike normal college freshmen's whose parents chaperoned their children as they settled into their new home to start their journey as college students, my parents left that to me. Robin speaks highly of her family, both her parents are wealthy lawyers. Though she was in the dorm room first she allowed me to pick the bed that I wanted. I told her it didn't matter to me, because in my mind sleeping on the floor was better than worrying about what time my father would be coming into my bed almost every night at his convenience. Robin and I were like-minded, she believed that her studies were the most important component to success as I did. Robin is a bit more talkative then I am. This girl made me talk to her, which was so annoying until it became funny; you couldn't help but like her. After getting all settled in I laid in my new bed thinking finally I am free. Yet, I worried about my younger sister LeAnn who was developing into a pre- teen hoping that my father wouldn't hurt her too. Poor Lena the last that I saw her she was sleeping on the street and refused to come home, but now I understand why. As I drifted off to sleep I knew it was out of my hands and prayer was no longer an option. Prayer in my mind was nothing but a bunch of babbling wishes to a fictitious god that cannot exist; and that was my new reality.

We had a few days before classes started so Robin and I decided to walk around to get familiar with the campus and meet some new people. Hanging out at the Student Union we met two nice girls named Candice and Shyla. They were both English majors, Candice was very intelligent but she liked to party to blow off steam as she says. Shyla on the other hand wasn't the party girl; she was more into working to pay for school. She came from a crime infested, poverty stricken project housing development in Chicago where violence had claimed the lives of two of her six brothers. However, she didn't allow her circumstances to dictate her future, and she was very cautious in disclosing that part of her life. This girl had her head together, she's President of one of the most prestigious Honor Societies, and deeply involved in student activities. Shyla was also the first person in her entire family to ever go to college, but she used her skills from the hood to get things done. She could turn it on and off like a faucet, from business to street, she definitely has the gift of gab and deems herself a hustler. How she did it was beyond me, but she was able to pull it off. Given the amount of respect she got from her peers and faculty alike, no one seemed to be on to her. We talked for hours and Shyla shared with us that she worked in a local strip club nearby. Shocked! I had heard about those kinds of clubs but never knew what really took place there. This started in her sophomore year and apparently this was how she'd been paying for her education. Shyla told us if she didn't dance she would have had to forfeit her education because she couldn't afford school. She also informed us that a lot of the girls in school worked at the club and that they are always looking for new talent. In my mind I am thinking is this chick trying to recruit us or something, because that's not going to fly with me. I am not knocking her for what she does, but, keep that over there Boo. Needless to say that gave me and Robin our topic of discussion before bed. Although Candice and Shyla were upper-classmen they were cool, so we all remained friends and hung out every chance we got. She extended an invitation to me and Robin to attend a Rush that eventually in our sophomore year led both of us to pledging and crossing over into the hottest Sorority on campus. We were proud to represent our sister "Shy" and the "Pink & Green", after she had successfully crossed over into becoming an alumni, and an active member of the corporate world.

I took on a full load 6 classes 4 days a week for a total of 18 credits for the first semester. Books, tuition, room and board along with a meal plan and the health insurance required took a huge chunk of my financial aid and scholarship money. I was covered for the first semester but the second semester I would have to work to offset the rest of my tuition cost. My parents wanted me to go to a local private Christian college where my tuition would have been completely covered because father was a pastor, and that would have also meant I would live at home and continue to be my dad's concubine. But until the day I walked out of their house I let them believe that I was going to the school of dad's choice. However, nothing could be further from the truth, and when I refused we had a huge argument and they cut me off completely. My freedom was the greatest gift that they ever gave because it sure trumped the life that they took from me. I was now free to do what I wanted and the first thing I did was change my wardrobe, got contact lenses, and let my hair down, "Literally".

My workload was rigorous from Calculus to Chemistry and several Psychology courses, my brain was on overload. After class sleep was not an option because I worked at the campus Daycare center for a few hours in the afternoon, and a full day on Friday when I didn't have classes. Pulling all night study sessions was an understatement, but between classes, studying, my job, and 2-3 hours of sleep I made it work. The holidays were going to be rough for me because I knew that I would be spending them alone. I just refused to go home. There had been absolutely no contact with my family in months and I really missed my sisters. Through it all I'd met some very nice people here in Georgia. My roommate Robin has become more like a sister, she often invited me to come home with her on some weekends and I refused every time. However, I decided to take her up on her offer to visit with her family for Christmas. The money to cover the entire Christmas break in a hotel and the cost for food was not feasible, especially since I'd just spent Thanksgiving alone at a nearby motel. Besides her parents were anxious to meet me and her mom was always so sweet. She'd send care packages for both Robin and me. It was the least I could do to show my gratitude to her family, and being lonely with my thoughts was no fun. We packed up for our trip to Atlanta, I had never been to that part of town before so I didn't know what to expect. Robin's dad came to pick us up. He was a very tall, handsome and distinguished gentleman, with a measure of confidence that made me stand up a little taller in his presence. In a deep baritone typed voice he asked. "Are you girls about ready to get on the road"? We both replied yes sir, he loaded our bags into the trunk of his car and we were off. Robin and her dad seemed to have a very close relationship. She was definitely a daddy's girl and the middle child like me. The 2 hour drive was interesting. Her dad asked a lot of questions as he watched me from the rear view mirror waiting for my response about my family. I guess he was curious as to why I wasn't spending Christmas with them, which made me very uncomfortable. It was like he knew something; I was anxious and a bit irritated. Robin must have sensed my discomfort and shifted the conversation in another direction. I was thinking "Good save girl" because it almost felt like a fucking interrogation to me. Turns out Mr. Coles was a very nice man; family oriented. His love for his wife and children were obvious, and that seemed to be all he spoke about. Finally, we arrived at this large beautiful house that looked more like a castle with lots of windows behind an electric gate. As we drove up and around the huge circular driveway which boast their own personal light show that screamed festive, I couldn't help but think all these people do is practice law? Shit maybe I should change my major if lawyers live like this. Georgia is unseasonably warm for December, but we are in the South. When we entered the palace's foyer of grandeur with a revolving chandelier, marble flooring and a massive double staircase that led to their own personal piece of heaven on earth, we were then greeted by the rest of the family. My thought process was on overdrive because I was witnessing what perfection looks like and how shallow my life must have been before now. The Coles family was absolutely the most beautiful family that I'd ever met. Especially Bryce,

Robin's older brother, he is taller than his father about 6'5. A perfectly chiseled piece of chocolate with a smile that left me spellbound. In an effort not to stare too hard and risk salivating like a crazed animal I quickly turned my focus to their 16 year old sister Renee. Mr. Coles continuously alluded to the fact that she was very intelligent. Like me, she too had smashed the SAT and ACT with perfect scores so Colleges and Universities were already knocking at their door. I also noticed right away that she was very sweet, not to mention cute. Mrs. Coles or "Mother" as they all so lovingly called her was breathtaking, she didn't look old enough to have adult children. Her perfectly caramel colored skin made her look as if she had been kissed by the sun; and she wore a short but sharp hairstyle that accentuated her almond shaped eyes and high cheekbones. It is apparent that she works out regularly the way her dress hugged every curve she owned. Mrs. Coles gave me the biggest and tightest hug I'd ever had, but it felt like she transferred something from her spirit to mine, then she looked me straight in my eyes and said welcome! Our home is your home My Dear.

After our initial meet and greet one of the servants showed me where I would be sleeping during my visit. I literally had my own private quarters in their home; along with my own servants attending to my personal needs. I thought to myself "Wow"! I didn't know how to receive all of these amenities. However, I couldn't seem to shake the feeling of the hug that I'd received from Mrs. Coles. It made me realize that I was in need of that unknown something that's missing from my life, but what could that be?

Robin comes in the room and startles me as I check out my surroundings to tell me to come down for dinner. As we walk down the long well lit grand hallways with something new and exciting to see in every room, it was like touring a museum. When we finally reached the dining quarters, it would be an insult to refer to it as a dining room I was amazed once again. The massive table with chairs for the royal family must have seated twenty or more and the art work was like none that I'd ever seen. Linen napkins, burning candles, silverware with a sturdy amount of weight on it, fine china and crystal along with freshly cut flowers adorned the table. When the servants bought out the four course meal consisting of a salad, entrée, the main course, followed by Tiramisu for desert, it felt more like I was dining in a fine restaurant. The presentation boasted a hint of fanfare, and while I was impressed I could tell that this was a part of their everyday lives. Then it happened, Mr. Coles said let us pray. My eyes rolled up into the back of my head as I thought here we go with this bullshit. I wasn't feeling it, prayer was a waste of breathe, with no real meaning. However, I could not be disrespectful in their home so I looked at the family and adopted the same posture as the rest of them. I bowed my head but didn't close my eyes. Watching and listening to him pray made me angry, why was I once again being subjected to this god? This was part of the reason that I vowed to never go home and chose not to go to a school that made references to god in any way.

Great! Now that the praying was over we started to eat the delicious dinner. I was so hungry but, watching them eat made me nervous, which of the many forks to choose from was the salad fork? How am I supposed to cut the steak? I just watched what they did and followed suit; it was like a game of "Simon Says" only I was secretly playing the rounds alone. The conversation was going nicely. I learned that the Coles family were big investors outside of owning their law firm, and they also owned a chain of very successful restaurants in and around Georgia. This would explain their wealth.

They discussed everything from school to politics to where they would take their annual family vacation, Hawaii was their choice. I thought it must be nice! But, what kind of family actually cares what the children think? This was something that I was not accustomed to in my house, and it was interesting to learn that some parents allowed their children to have a voice in family matters. For some reason I couldn't stop looking at Bryce he was very handsome, a grad student also studying law at a prestigious University set to graduate in the upcoming spring. I felt a sense of guilt and disgust for my being attracted to him, after all I was still in love with Vincent. Could my father be right about me? Do I have whore like tendencies, and does this explain why I am attracted to more than one guy at the same time?

In the midst of all of these thoughts taking place in my head it happens. Robin's little sister Renee asked about my family. So Lorraine where are you from, how many siblings do you have, what do your parents do for a living and why aren't you spending Christmas with them? I no longer thought she was sweet nor cute just nosey as hell. Robin saves the day once again girl stop asking so many questions. Then out of the blue Bryce says, it's nice to have you here celebrating the holidays with us Lorraine. Maybe

47

you can join us for our summer vacation and the family quickly agreed. With a sort of grimace on my face I replied, my summer will be consumed with work. Bryce had a sneaky yet sexy look in his eyes and he responds as he cut through his steak, "You can't work all the time, and a little play time is good for everyone including you Lorraine". Embarrassed and a bit taken a back I smiled. Was he flirting with me? Whatever it was I liked it.

Dinner came to a close and we reconvened to the Great Room for cocktails. The Coles family with the exception of Renee had red wine to drink. But, what they didn't know was I'd never had a drink in my life. The closest that I'd been to real wine would be the grape juice served in church on every fourth Sunday during Holy Communion. They all shared their future plans and after my second glass I loosened up enough to share a bit of my own. One by one the spirit of sleep mixed with semi intoxication fell on everybody, and when Robin finally left the room Bryce and I were alone. We had a couple more glasses of wine and continued our conversation. But, I was about to find out if he had been flirting with me earlier at the dinner table in front of his entire family.

Indeed there was no doubt that this was a complete crack on me. In a very deep, and sexy tone he asked "Do you have a boyfriend". That's personal don't you think? He moved in closer "You like me don't you" biting his bottom lip. Smiling out of sheer drunken nervousness all I could think was this dude is too sure of himself. But he was right, and I replied "What difference does that make"? He moved in really close invading my personal space and kissed me on the lips. I pulled back, but I wanted more. His lips were very soft and he smelled incredible. Suddenly the touch of a man no longer gave me that feeling of crawling skin, all I felt were chills and a tingling sensation that made my panties wet. Curiosity coupled with the four glasses of wine catapulted me to the next level. I didn't care, I wanted this man from the time that I first laid my eyes on him just a few short hours ago. He was so gentle, kissing the back of my neck until the hairs seemed to stand at attention. But, that wasn't the only thing at attention, his manpower was large and stiff rubbing against my leg. I was experiencing Arrhythmia as my heart raced into overdrive. This man worked on my body with such passion that I didn't realize that he'd gotten my clothes off. It was like I was in some sort of erotic induced coma that caused me to slip in and out of consciousness at his will. What I do remember is him gently sucking and slightly biting my nipples and they were just as erect as he was. Leaving a tingling, warm yet cool sensation when he blew his breath on them that radiated downward causing a throbbing stimuli, leaving my panties drenched with desire. Kissing and licking my body from my neck down to my belly button with such sensuality. So gone with pleasure my legs parted with ease to the point of collapse to allow him to kiss my inner thighs. But, just when I thought life couldn't get any better than this he did something that had never been done. He kissed my pussy, and extreme euphoria took control over my body, and that shit rendered me speechless for a moment.

Bryce neglected to tell me that he too was also a musician. He used his tongue as a device to pluck my clitoris until I began to softly sing erotic soprano. Just as I felt the climax building he would shift to a very soft sucking motion, and blow gently, but just enough to allow my body to calm down, then he took my clitoris between his teeth and sucked so vigorously while allowing in just enough air that it caused a vicious vibration that made me explode. This was my very first orgasm and it felt like I was dying a slow pleasurable death, slipping so quickly that the lack of oxygen to my brain caused me to experience a dizzy spell. While I was losing my mind with ecstasy he licked, kissed, and sucked my inner thighs allowing me to catch my breath. But as soon as I began to regain control over my body he'd hit me with that vaginal vibration that caused me to cum over and over again. He controlled how much and how many times I would cum. In an attempt to tap-out, he said "NO" so I grabbed one of his mother's very expensive throw pillows to use as a shield to muffle my screams of pleasure bought on by the overpowering state of ecstasy. This man caused a spewing from my orifice that sent my nervous system into orbit. Legs shaking out of control; Bryce was responsible for this new found pleasure that felt larger than life. He gave me my first orgasm, or should I say my first set because there were multiples. When he finished feasting he came up and stared straight into my eyes with his big brown ones and informed me that I was a squirter. In awe with his performance but, what was he wearing on his chin? It was my essence, and he kissed me as he fed it back to me. I have to admit I taste good, kind of sweet. Bryce flipped me over to my knees, pushed my head to the couch cushion, gripped my 23 inch waist and pressed his thumbs in the small of my lower back just above my dimples. This caused my back to form a deep arch, and with the thrust of a locomotion; he hid himself inside of me. We both sighed as if we had been waiting our entire lives for this feeling. Bryce had no idea that I was finally having sex at my own free will and that although I wasn't a virgin, he was my first and it was phenomenal. It felt like I was having an outer body experience. However, he was indeed the experienced one, but I was about to learn something about myself. Bryce spoke softly into my ear "Get on Top". The vibration from his masculine voice surged through my soul. I'd never done this before of course, but I felt invincible. Passion to the point of sheer nasty took charge because I rode this man using every motion and speed possible, and I could feel his dick stiffening and pulsating. With my back facing him, he used his left hand to grip my waist tightly, then he wrapped his right hand around my long hair as if it were a rein of a stallion and pulled hard enough, but gentle enough that he stayed in control of the ride. I felt like we were the only two people in this world. When I turned to face him, he made me realize that I too had power, sort of the way I felt when Vincent kissed me for the first time. The look in his eyes, him biting his bottom lip, the moans that roared from him loins, and the dazed look on his face turned me on. I began to ride him with a fervency that pulled every ounce of his strength and we both released and oozed with ecstasy in the same space in time. It was the most remarkable experience in my life.

Hours had passed as we laid together and talked until just before the sun started to rise. Bryce is really cool and was pretty transparent with me about his life, he was a bit candid at times which was really funny. I felt like we'd known each other forever, not just for hours. We talked about so many things, including what he meant about me being a squirter. When he explained I was so embarrassed but, he convinced me that it was a good thing. He said most women did not have the ability to express their sexual pleasures outwardly, LITERALLY! We laughed together about my new found erotic talent. Bryce also had a serious side to him; he and I shared many of the same views on life, career, and family. He played in my hair and rambled on about my beauty. Why don't you have a boyfriend? My education takes precedence over everything. He said I do understand your level of focus, that's the same drive my parents instilled in us as children. Though my family background was completely different, for some reason I felt a sense of validation from this man, and that further heightened my attraction to him. The sun started to appear, we both agreed to keep this a secret. We rushed back to our quarters before anyone woke up to discover us. Muscles rippling this fool walked away with my panties tucked between his pearly white teeth, pants undone, belt buckle falling off to the side, giving a slight view of the cutest ass I'd ever seen and shirtless because I was wearing his button up to cover my nakedness. There was only one problem "I fell in Love".

The beginning of my junior year was going well; it was a bit more expensive to live in the dorms so I found an apartment off campus. Robin and I were closer than ever, I had really become a part of their family. However, Bryce and I were closer than anyone in the family could ever imagine. We had been secretly seeing each other for more than a year now, the sex was absolutely mind boggling and we always used condoms because we didn't want any slip-ups. Bryce passed the Bar exam shortly after we met and is successfully practicing Law with his parent's firm. He takes care of all of my living expenses and helps with school. We go on trips alone and he gave me the down payment to buy my first new car. The holidays were nice with Robin's family but, something about me and Bryce's secret seemed to make it that much sweeter. Sneaking off to have sex in the bathroom, laundry quarters, on their boat and even his parent's bed while the family were only steps away gave us the sense of excitement and danger. I did feel a bit guilty when Robin would visit my apartment and I knew her brother was coming over to stay the night with me. I'd give her some lame ass excuse so she'd leave. Surprisingly they never ran into one another. They'd sometimes literally miss each other by seconds almost but, he floats my boat so anything for my perfectly chiseled piece of chocolate. Even giving him head became one of my favorite things to do for him, it gave me complete control. At first my lack of experience left him with unwanted teeth marks and gagging to the point of almost vomiting, that was kind of fucked up and funny at the same time; but he allowed me to practice on him whenever I wanted to, and he was a great coach. However, it wasn't long before I perfected my knob slobbering skills; and when I put in that work he could no longer control the flow. The peach trick is one of his favorites. I would get a big juicy Georgia peach that's soft yet firm enough for me to carve out the core and seed, cut it down so it covers only half of his manpower. Slide it on his dick and jerk him off while sucking and stroking until he bust the hardest nut that he could, and the taste of the peach mixed with his cum that

I always swallowed was a delectable treat for me. That shit works every time. I laid claim to that dick, and he had no problem admitting that it was mine. Bryce became very protective and there was nothing that he wouldn't do for me. I felt so safe, it was as if we were in marital bliss without being married. What we had was good but my emotions are beginning to require more of him. I never wanted him to leave my presence and when my phone rang like clockwork at 6 am, 12 noon, and 6pm I got chills because I knew it was my "Boo Thang" on the other end of the phone. His touch comforted me and he could read my mind. After making love he would hold me so close that his heartbeat would rock me to sleep. I could think about something and he would speak it. It was as if he were a prophet or had some sort of mystical powers. Or it could just be the power of "THE D". Everything is perfect so why couldn't we just share our love with the world and his family? Although we never really spoke the words outwardly, I loved him, he adored me and when we were together our actions demonstrated our love for each other. I kept telling myself not to complicate things by allowing my feelings to get in the way. He made me happy and that was more than I'd had since my high school sweetheart so I better just leave it at that.

It has been almost four years since I'd seen or heard from any of my family members. I wondered how my sisters were doing, but I never reached out to them and they didn't contact me either. Graduation was around the corner and like the bastard that fathered me I was graduating Summa Cum Laude. I'd also done very well on the MCAT's and gained acceptance into an elite club for test takers who score in the top 1%, this also provided me with the acceptance to the Medical school of my choice located in California. Although I'd accomplished all of this academic success, and things were not good between my parents and me, I still felt badly that they wouldn't be sharing this very special moment in my life like the rest of my peers in the graduating class of 1992. Robin's family was there to cheer me on as if I were their own child and it felt good to have had their support; so it turned out to be a great day. We went out for dinner to celebrate, but I could not help reflecting back on my life. It seemed that my family never had that special something that I saw in the Coles family. Being on my own taught me that what I'd learned from my family wasn't absolute truth. The clothes I wore, the corky glasses, tight hair bun and the whole puritan girl lifestyle that amounted to total disaster. I realized that my life before now was nothing more than a skillfully exploited situation to maintain a certain image for the church. But, somehow spending time with the Coles family helped me understand the hug that Mrs. Coles gave me a few years ago. It provided me with a well-balanced dose of love that I'd never received from my own mother. Mrs. Coles served as sort of a surrogate to a motherless child, and I love her for that.

I had not seen Bryce since my graduation day, just our regularly scheduled phone calls that I'd received for the last several years. He has been tied up in meetings and busy working on a big case that would land him a partnership with the firm. Travel has also been on his long list of things to do, but he promised that he would make it up to me. Standing at my living room window relaxing, and drinking a glass of sweet red wine, staring out at the blue sky thinking about my move to California for Medical School. Pondering over me and Bryce's conversation on how we were going to make this relationship thing work long distance when my phone rings. It's Robin, asking what you doing Sissy? Nothing much. Are you coming home with me next weekend? It had become the norm for me to go to their house with or even without her. I asked what's going on next weekend. What Robin said next snatched my breath away. "Bryce is getting married". It felt like the world was coming to an end, everything was moving in slow motion. The glass slipped from my hand and shattered all over the floor, red wine soiled my white draperies, I could barely breathe. The pace of my heartbeat doubled and I felt physically sick. Robin called my name a few times, and when I finally answered I was trembling with disbelief. Desperately trying to pull my shit together so she wouldn't suspect anything to ask the questions who, when and why haven't I ever met, seen, or heard about this girl. Why hadn't you ever mentioned her to me? Robin went on to say because it wasn't worth talking about, and Trina was a girl that he has been dating long distance for the past five years, and she was also an attorney. The family had only met her once or twice and they all think she's a snobby Bitch that intentionally kept her distance. In a silent frenzy with myself I told her that I would call her back. All I could think was this can't be happening to me; all this time and this man never even mentioned another woman. My legs collapsed out from under me and my body went limp as I slid down the living room wall blinded by my tears. Heart riddled with pain and no understanding of this part of my life. I was physically sick and ran to the bathroom to throw up. I loved Bryce so much, and he'd become the source of my satisfaction. It didn't seem real and the more I thought about it the sicker I felt. My emotions ranged from hurt to rage, but as I combed through the details of our relationship I began to realize just how he was able to get over on me. Yes we did spend a lot of time together but, I'd only been to his place a few times. We spent most of our time at his parent's house, my apartment or out of town. The scheduled phone calls, and even his recent absence made more sense to me now. I felt so stupid, and I was pissed off.

I grabbed the phone to call him, and when he answered I asked him in a calm yet sarcastic tone, so who is Trina and when were you going to tell me that you're getting married? There was a brief moment of silence until this Negro got snide and completely raw with his words. Needless to say the fight was on and we had some choice words for each other. Bryce told me that what we had was purely sexual and that he never promised me anything more than that. He expressed that I could've walked away at any time. Overwhelmed with shock thinking, who is this man that I'd given myself to all this time? Damn, he made me feel like I was nothing more than his whore for hire for the past several years? But he was right, and it was obvious that I was in love alone based on the shit that he was saying to me. But what in the fuck happened to the sweet guy that held me tightly and never let me fall when things got bad, he use to make me feel safe? Speechless because I knew it was over, no apologies he just informed me that he wouldn't bother me again, and that I shouldn't contact him anymore. In an instant that chapter and season of my life was over and devastation set in once again. Why wasn't I good enough to be his wife, and until now I was sure that one day I would be although he never said it. I was sure that I was truly happy, but now that Bryce is gone to spend forever with his new wife the pain along with my past issues were back smothering out what little life I had left over.

Moving to another state couldn't have come at a better time, and was the best thing for me after losing whatever I thought I had with Bryce. California would give me a fresh start and I had enough money in my savings to get a new apartment and pay the rent for six months. Although Bryce was a no good bastard his monetary generosity over the last few years gave me some cushion. But I was faced once again with the difficulty of how to pay for Medical school. I took a job waiting tables in a local diner right off the coast, and the view of the beach is beautiful. However, I would need another job to supplement my income to pay my car note, and insurance along with everything that comes along with survival. Being in California took me back to a conversation that I had with my first love and high school sweetheart Vincent. We were planning to buy our forever home here and live out a perfect life together yet the thought now made me sad and I wondered what happened to him? Is he happy living out his dreams, and I really hoped so because my life was in disarray.

Classes were beginning and I'd gotten registered, hitting the books like the scholar I am to keep my mind off of my troubles. Robin and I are still close and my love for her is still more like a sister, but I have to admit it is painful talking to her. She rambles on about the family and to hear her talk about her brother makes me sick to my stomach. It became necessary for me to cut our phone conversations short or avoid them altogether to maintain my sanity. The last thing that I needed to hear is Bryce and his new wife are having a baby or some shit like that. Robin had become my best friend but I couldn't share my heart or pain with her. What was becoming of my life? I seemed to be living a lie and drowning in secrets that made me feel like a prisoner. Everything that made me happy eventually turned my world upside down. The only two friends that I'd ever had were in the dark about who I really was, and they knew nothing about the internal or external damage that I lived with. However, unlike my best friends I suffered in silence.

I am the gatekeeper of my friend's most intimate thoughts and feelings, but who would be my gatekeeper? My relationship with Bryce made me want to give love another chance; it made me think that love could be a beautiful part of life that everyone deserved. But now I'm back at square one, FUCK LOVE! I don't believe in that bullshit anymore. Anything that hurts this bad can't be right. I tried it but it failed me over and over. My dad, my mom, Bryce, and even god failed me. The thought of all of this made me angry and bitter. I told myself that love is merely a metaphor used by bullies to crush, smash and destroy the lives of good people. I vowed never to try it again, and have decided to just live out whatever life I had left doing what's needed to get by. Maybe my dream of becoming a Psychiatrist is merely to help me understand what makes me tick, and hopefully I can recover someday.

Medical School is rigorous but so is everything else in my life. Of course the help from Bryce stopped and I am struggling to make ends meet. California is very expensive so my waitressing job isn't cutting it. My mind revisited the conversation that I'd had with Shyla a few years ago when I'd first started Undergrad in Georgia. Was stripping something I wanted? No, but I had to do what I had to do. After some research on the matter, I went to a local

Gentlemen's Club that was considered high class if that analogy really exist in such a place. Reluctantly I walked in to meet the owner Tony, and inquired about becoming a dancer. I thought that I would have to audition, and that made me a bit uncomfortable. But, he took one look at me and asked me to turn around so he could check me out. I guess my very curvaceous body frame was enough to convince him that I was a good fit for his club, because his next question was when can you start? Desperate I replied as soon as possible. Okay come by tonight to check out how things operate. Tuesday's are usually pretty slow so it would be a perfect time to get an idea of how things work here. He introduced me to some of the girls that were practicing, most of them barely spoke, just rolled their eyes and kept dancing. However, Domonique whose stage name is "Juicy" was the main girl at the club; she's beautiful and had a big ass and nice perky titties, so her stage name made perfect sense.

Tony told her to teach me the ropes of working in his club. Domonique gave me her number and told me to call her when I had some free time, but not before she gave me the stink eye. I was really intimidated, and when I called her later that day the first thing she wanted to know was why I was dancing in the first place? Domonique also said, I mean you seem like a really smart girl that should be working in the corporate world. I explained my financial situation concerning school, and she said I guess we all got our own fucked up reason for doing this shit. But, okay. We met up and she took me so I could get shoes and some costumes. I invested my last $150.00 and got my first pair of stilettos and a very skimpy outfit, a red bra and throngs to match. I told her that I wasn't much of a dancer so she came back to my place and we rearranged the furniture and practiced for a couple of hours. She did moves that I'd never seen in my life and I could not mimic any of them. She said, OKAY GIRL! So you're not much of a dancer but can you "FUCK"? Shocked, and Embarrassed I didn't know where she was going with that question, so I said what does that have to do with anything? She said in this business it means everything. I quickly asked they don't expect me to sleep with these men do they? She said no but that's strictly up to you. Thinking to myself what in the hell have I gotten myself into with this? Domonique said, you got the look and if you get the moves you will get the paper. Dumb, so I asked, what paper? She said girl you are so new! But, hang with me and I will help you lose that green cloud hanging over your head, because it's that cloud that will get you late in this business. I 'm talking about money. Then she asked with almost an attitude, SO IMMA ASK YOU AGAIN; WHY YOU DOING THIS ANYWAY? But, before I could speak a word she cut me off and facetiously said, Oh! I know, you in college and can't pay for it ain't you? So let's work. You got something to drink? Yeah you want water, soda or juice? OH MY GOD GIRL, YOU THE DAMN GREEN GOBBLIN. NO! Child do you have anything to help you relax like liquor? OH! I have some wine, she ask, so you don't have anything stronger? Just like that Domonique went in her purse and pulled out a bottle of liquor and informed me that this was her emergency stash. I said that's the hard stuff, and she said Yep! This will loosen you up. I grabbed two glasses, and she poured. When I sipped it was the nastiest thing I'd ever tasted, she said no girl knock that shit back, and so I inhaled and knocked it back as she said. My chest burned like hell, but within five minutes I felt like I could do anything. After I finished with the drunken giggling spell that I was having, she put on some slow music and started to dance very seductively. I watched her moves and I began to second guess myself, this girl could really dance. No wonder she was the top dancer at the club. Then she said do what I do, so I proceeded to try and failed miserably. Irritated, Domonique stopped the music and

66

asked in a high pitched tone, TELL ME WHY YOU
DOING THIS AGAIN? I said to pay for my education. She
asked what is it you want to become? A Psychiatrist, then
she said well first lesson, you need to control your thoughts
because, if you are going to be a doctor you must first be a
dancer. She asked "Now How Bad do You Want It"? I
replied really badly. Juicy instructed me to close my eyes,
and as she stood so closely behind me, with her body
pressed firmly against mine, she whispered in my ear
saying, move your body like you did when you fucked the
last dude you were in love with. Immediately my emotions
flared at the thought of Bryce but, the alcohol helped me to
release all of my inhibitions and before I knew it I was
dancing just as seductively as she could. Domonique placed
me in front of my mirrored covered wall and I saw
someone new. She was sexy, sensual, and ready to get that
money. We practiced for a couple of hours then we
discussed what my stage name would be. I asked why I
couldn't use my own name. Domonique said the first rule
of this game is to keep your personal life totally separate
from the work place. Your job is to fulfill the fantasy that's
it in the customer's minds; by using your body to trigger
their pheromones causing them to release that money into
your pockets. I thought to myself Wow! It was interesting

how she explained that. Maybe because I was studying animal and human behavior, and their functions it gave me a clearer understanding of her analogy. But, I couldn't think of anything as far as a stage name. Then Dominique Said I Got It! Your hourglass shaped figure reminds me of a Silhouette, so that will be your new stage name. I said cool with me! Wow! "Silhouette", the more I pondered the name and its meaning, the more I thought to myself how metaphorically creative. The name was so befitting because I never wanted anyone to see what I was hiding underneath the black mask that concealed all of my secrets. This stage name allowed me to continue to hide the woman inside of me that had been shattered into a million pieces. Displeased at what I was about to do yet, I had no other choice if I was going to accomplish my goal of becoming a doctor. I'd come too far to throw it all away now. We worked on my dance skills for a week, and it turned out that I was a better dancer than I'd originally thought I was. Juicy focused on teaching me a routine that we would perform together my first time out. I also hung at the club watching Juicy, and getting familiar with how things worked. I somehow managed to do all of this between classes, my studies and my other job. Finally, I was about to make my debut at one of The Classiest Gentleman's clubs in California. My first time dancing and I was performing on stage, this was not the norm. New girls have to work their way to that point. But, Juicy felt that if she and I did a set my first time out, it would give me the advantage that I needed to be successful here. Because she was the top girl at the club her request never went unanswered with the owner Tony. But, this would later cause some unwanted jealously between the other girls and me. Terrified, Dominque or should I say Juicy gave me a pep talk, continuously reminding me about the reason I was doing this in the first place. We took a shot then she said "LETS GO MAKE THIS MONEY DOCTOR GIRL". The DJ played our first song a mixture of Hip Hop and upbeat tunes that got everybody in the club hyped up. He introduced Juicy as the Notorious Pussy Popper, and announced me as the New Sensual, Sexy, and Sweet Tasting Silhouette. I picked up my head and boldly did my "Bad Bitch Walk" out onto the stage for the first time, and with every step I took my ass bounced, and the crowd went wild. We did our set, using the, seductive sounds of Janet J. There was a lot of lewd suggestions of sensual girl touching and teasing, we were giving the crowd what they wanted; and the money flowed like rain. The room was low lit with flashing lights and packed to capacity, filled with both men and women. The music thumped so hard that I could feel the bass pumping in my chest causing a vibration. The sound of clinking glasses, and beer bottles coupled with smoke and howling Horny men made me think of the Hell that my father preached about. For a split second I thought about God but, the fact that I was in this place made the thought dissipate as quickly as it came. Because if god was so real why had I not seen him in my life. Titties and ass everywhere, lap dances, girls floating around the room looking for dudes or females to entertain, this place was jumping. Only the top girls like Juicy performed on the stage, and they made the most money. Men threw so much money at the stage performers, but these girls had to work extra hard for it. After my debut performance the crowd couldn't get enough. Everybody seemed to want a piece of me. Overwhelmed, I found myself standing in a dark corner and everything seemed to be moving in slow motion, when this dude gently grabbed my hand and ask me to dance for him. He pulled up a chair and had a seat, the alcohol had really kicked in, and so I closed my eyes and proceeded to perform my very first lap dance. I let myself go and danced for my life; this dude put so much money in my bra, garter belt, and G-string and I was amazed that I was really able to make money as a stripper.

Before I knew it I was working the room with ease. When I proceeded to walked away from one guy another was tugging on my hand. I danced for a few hours as my girl Juicy watched my back. After about four hours I went to the dressing room where Juicy and some of the other girls told me how well I did for my first time. The owner Tony must have thought I was good for his business because he was really pushing for me to work at least 5-6 days a week. I told him that I would let him know for certain tomorrow. Some of the girls were counting their money, and Juicy gave me my cut for the set that we performed together. I stuffed all my money in a bag without counting it, and got dressed to go home because I had classes in a few short hours. The drive home was interesting, it felt so surreal. I could not believe what I had just done. I ran in the house stripping off my clothes at the door in a hurry to take a shower. After washing off the stench of club life I dumped my money on the bed and proceeded to count it. To my surprise I'd made a little more than $500.00 in just a few short hours. I wasn't proud of the job but it damn sure paid the bills. I made enough money to get all of my books in just a few short hours. Needless to say I quit the waitressing job to work the club fulltime. This new found career path had me grossing some $5200.00 a month or more.

Domonique and I became close friends, she was a single mother with two young children a girl and boy. She dropped out of school in the 10th grade to have her first daughter, and she had her son four years later when she was 19. Their father married her when he found out they were having a second baby. He was an older guy that owned a couple of businesses, and a big drug dealer that had been set up by his best friend, and the god-father of their children. Her husband was shot and killed execution style while she was still pregnant with their son. However, he'd bought her a beautiful home that was completely paid for in the Hills, and left her some money. She still owned his clothing store but it wasn't doing as well as she had hoped, and Domonique wasn't educated on how to run it. But, to maintain the lifestyle that her children were accustomed to, without tapping too much into the money that her husband left her, dancing became a supplemental income to pay for her children to continue their private school education and extra-curricular activities. So like me she was basically working the club for the same reason that I was. Domonique told me that was the reason she wanted to help me, because I was trying to make a better life for myself. I looked at her differently after that. In the club she was a beast but, as a mom she was a phenomenal classy woman that wanted the best for her children, and fought quite hard to provide for them. I gave her some tips on how to better operate her business in hopes that the store would not fold. Domonique was grooming me to be her protégé, and I was quickly becoming a hot commodity in the club. She told me that she was doing a bachelor party at a hotel and asked if I wanted to dance? Domonique always gave me first dibs at every opportunity to make some extra money, and she could only take 6 girls. Afraid I asked would that be safe since we wouldn't have bodyguards like we do at the club. Domonique looked me in the eyes and shouted "DO YOU THINK I WOULD GO ANYWHERE THAT WAS NOT SAFE, I HAVE MY BABIES TO GO HOME TO". She went on to say, I know the guy throwing the party. Still a bit leery; I said let me think about it because I have an important test coming up. This would be my first private party and some of the other girls were jealous. It was a Friday night and the party was in the Penthouse of a fancy five star hotel. I had a very important exam to study for, but I liked the idea of the extra money. I decided to cram and go do the party. Shit I could always use more money. I called to tell her I was coming, grabbed my bag filled with my dance shoes, costumes, good smelling oils, and makeup, snatched my keys off the table and made a mad

73

dash to the door. We all met in the lobby of this grand hotel; when we got on the elevator I felt fear taking over. I wanted to run back to my car and go home but I couldn't. I would be putting her in a bad spot if I pulled out at the last minute, and she had been the most down to earth and real person that I'd ever encountered, outside of my old friend Kia. So I pulled my shit together and put my big girl thongs on thinking let's do this. I could hear the music as we got closer to the top floor, the elevator door opened directly to the penthouse itself. We were greeted by an older guy who was very respectful. Damn! The place had wall to wall window with an amazing view of the city. Domonique said we are getting dressed in this room on the left. My mind was all over the place, I could hear more men arriving. I asked Domonique who the groom was and she said the guy who greeted us was the groom's father but she didn't really know the groom. After about 30 minutes someone knocked on the door to let us know that the man of the hour had arrived, and we could get started. Nervous as hell because I had no idea what to expect, the girls filled me in and one by one they left the room. As the music played I could hear the men roaring like a pack of lions fighting over their "Pride". After about ten minutes and a few stiff drinks I decided to come out to make my first private party debut. This was a very diverse group of men but they all had something in common, great success and money. Stockbrokers, Engineers, Doctors, and Lawyers, you name it young and old but still very respectful so I was able to calm my fears. These men were throwing money at the girls like it was nothing, and not just dollar bills but 10's and even 20's so I got to work. It seemed I received the same response from this crowd at the party as I did my first time dancing in the club, everybody wanted a piece of me. When the Best man saw me, he took my hand yelling, All Yeah! Where is the groom, she is exactly what he needs. From behind the groom had a nice body but, when he turned around the face almost put me in total shock. His friend put my hand into his and his eyes scanned me from the bottom working his way up and his smile turned into sheer surprise Lorraine! He said. I wanted to die right in the spot that I was standing in; it was my first love Vincent. My heart skipped beats at the shock, and embarrassment. He quickly pulled me off to the side as his friends cheered him on not realizing there was a reunion taking place. As swiftly as he pulled me to the side, my girl Juicy was right there ready to handle her business. I assured her that I knew him very well and that it was okay. He took me in the other room and hugged me so tightly. I held on but not for long. He looked at me with such perplexity and asked what happened to you and how is it that you are dancing now? Mortified I told him that was none of his business. He smiled and hugged me again and said you were the last person that I ever expected to see, but if I could have been granted one wish it would have been to see you. I was thrilled to see him too, but the fact that he was getting married made me sad. I knew life had to go on but this could not be really happening. What were the odds that I would run into Vincent like this? I quickly put on my game face and we begin to talk, his boys and Juicy kept coming to the door. I guess they thought we were having sex and Juicy wanted to be sure that I was good. Once I came to the door still fully dressed in my bra and thong and explained to her that he was an old friend she left me alone. At least for a while, time went by and we never went back into the party room, it was getting late and we could hear some of his boys leaving. I told Juicy that I know about the girl code; never leave your girl behind. But I assured her that I was in good hands and that I would call her in the morning; so all the girls left the party, but not before Juicy threatened to chop Vincent's head off if anything happened to me. We all had a good laughed and she left us alone. The conversation was a bit awkward, so to break the ice I asked, so who's the lucky girl that's marrying the successful Chemical Engineer? Vincent told me that they met in college and she is an Accountant. He further explained that she was a very nice girl and that he loved her. I proceeded to wish him well when he interrupted, to tell me that he never stopped loving me and that he thought about me all the time. He also said that I was the girl that got away but not because he let me go, but because I wanted to go. I was flattered but, my heart was filled with a lot of pain. I was happy that he had found love again but, a bit jealous and pissed off that the opportunity was taken away from me by my own damn father. My hatred towards my dad was fueled even the greater at that moment. I told him that I was glad that his dreams were coming true; then he said it. Lorraine I still love you and if you give me the chance I will not get married. I stopped him in mid-sentence and told him that I would never do that to another person. I refuse to be responsible for that kind of pain, he asked what about my pain you left me and I still don't know why. I replied Vincent, life has taught me that we may not ever get the answers to certain questions nor do we always need them. Let's leave well enough alone. He finally accepted what I was saying and we continued our conversation. Needless to say we laughed about old times but, I guess he had to ask the question.

"Lorraine what happen to us"? "Did you really love me back then"? I was speechless because there was still a space in my heart for him, and he deserved an honest answer, but I couldn't give it to him. I politely skipped the subject; he took a deep breath and said, "Same Old Lorraine" we both laughed. Lying in the bed on our sides, face to face he kissed me on my forehead. Boy you better stop, or did you forget that you will be a married man in a few hours. He said I know; I just want to kiss you the way we weren't allowed to back in the day. I replied well nobody controls what I do now except me. He asked, so can I kiss you? Yes, one kiss. This was actually the kiss that I'd been waiting for, the kiss that added no fear, the kiss that I didn't have to hide. He moved closer and his lips touched mine and it felt just the way I imagined it would. Those old feelings begin to surface, but that voice inside of my head said "Lorraine you cannot get caught up in your emotions because it always ends up in heartbreak". So I turned back to my stone like self with a hint of selfishness attached. I climbed on top of him and looked into his beautiful green eyes with the intentions of much more than a kiss. I took off what little bit of clothes I had on to seduce him. Vincent could not resist because he was looking at that shy girl that he loved so much in high school completely naked. But, the

78

thought was totally barbaric in my mind, so I undressed him. He was lost with surprise at the shift in my slightly aggressive behavior that now left him speechless. I took complete control and advantage of him. His penis was as pretty as he was, long, thick, slightly curved to the left, stiff, and ready to be massaged. I performed oral sex on him but, it was different because I got so much pleasure watching his response, as I didn't neglect any portion of his precious piece of HARDWARE. Giving close attention to the shaft, and exploring the entire anatomy using my tongue as a tickling device, and as I properly moved his piece to the back of my throat swallowing him up until his dick was invisible. Then gently sucking on my way down and up again until I released him back into clear view, just to make him disappear again, it was magic. Apparently my experience with Bryce the bastard was really paying off. Vincent had a bit of aggressiveness built up inside also because, he placed his hands under my armpits and dragged my naked body up to his face leaving my own trail of wet secretions from my pussy on his stomach and chest. My legs were wide open as I sat in his face, gripping the headboard trying to control the moans that were damn near screams working like poetry at the multiple orgasms bought on by nature. Comprised of five then seven then five moans that seemed to be coming in rhythmical successions like a haiku. My body was shaking out of control when Vincent put one of his masculine arms around my petite waist and swiftly flipped me on my back, my legs resting on his shoulders, all while he's still holding, licking and sucking my labium minus structure that housed my clitoris in his warm wet mouth. He did not stop until he struck my climatic gold mine. I squirted leaving my nectar in his face, he used the bed sheet to wipe the essence of me from his mouth. But, just enough to kiss me, as he put my feet in the folds of his armpits only allowing my neatly polished toes to rest on his chest, while using his weight to press my thighs firmly on to the mattress. He looked me directly in my eyes telling me that he loved me, then he introduced his masculinity to my femininity for the very first time. That position allowed him to reach the bottom of my pussy, and yes he filled me up completely. I was rustling with my emotions, but my tear ducts where full to the point of overflowing with passion and I could not control the flow. In an effort to try and hide the tears I turned my head and closed my eyes. He whispered in my ear asking, tell the truth, you love me too I can feel it Lorraine. I refused to verbalize, I let my body language continue to speak for me. However, I had to separate my emotion of passion because

80

Download our app
or sign up at
PandaRewards.com

Claim exclusive
offers just for you

Unlock a surprise
gift every month^

Receive a Birthday
Gift from us

Earn 10 Panda Points**
for every $1 spent

New

PANDA REWARDS™

JOIN TODAY

GET A WELCOME GIFT*

GOOD FORTUNE ★ AWAITS

Descarga nuestra app o regístrate en PandaRewards.com

Recibe ofertas exclusivas solo para ti

Desbloquea un regalo sorpresa* cada mes*

Obtén un regalo* de cumpleaños

Gana 10 Panda Points** por cada $1

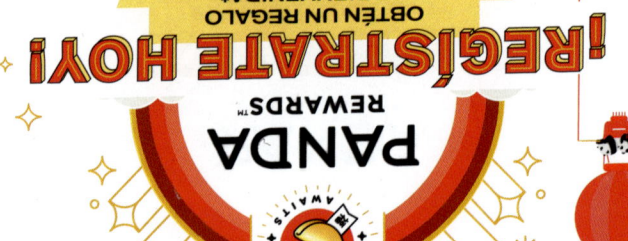

Nuevo

PANDA REWARDS™

¡REGÍSTRATE HOY!

OBTÉN UN REGALO DE BIENVENIDA*

GOOD FORTUNE AWAITS

this man will be in another bed this time tomorrow with his new wife. I had to let go of the fact that my first love was exploring my inner most secret place that had been tainted. Yet, it was so right and different, even from what I thought was good with Bryce. This felt special and my heart was broken once again that this would be the last encounter with my first encounter with the man of my dreams. It was in that moment my mindset changed. I understood that love did exist, only in tiny increments of my life and, I was experiencing it for the very first time. But once again, he deserved better than me. I allowed him into my intimate space and he was completely transparent with me. Vincent looked me straight in my eyes as they were filled with tears a sort of Deja vu of what happened in high school. He asked me once again if I would give him a chance to give me what he'd always wanted to give to me. LOVE! My heart bled as I told him to marry the woman that is somewhere happy that in a few hours she will own the rights and the patent to your last name. I turned my back and he held on to me tightly as I wished that I was in her shoes. He eventually fell asleep but, I stayed awake knowing I had to make him let me go. The sun lit the sky to symbolize the morning; I kissed him on the forehead, wishing him well in his new life. He walked me to the door we said our goodbyes. Yet, the tables were turned a bit because now I was hurting as he watched me walk away because I really wanted to stay.

Overwhelmed I tried to hold back the tears but, they were breaking through as I attempted to rush to my car so no one would witness the meltdown that was quickly escaping my body. The pain was too much to bear; the lump in my throat, the heaviness in my chest, and the tremors that wouldn't allow me to use my keys to open my car door. I was falling apart with pain and frustration, when I finally got in the car, slammed the door and looked back at the rooftop where Vincent was waiting for me if I wanted him, and I lost my mind. I laid my head on the steering wheel and cried for almost an hour, fighting with the decision to run back to him and ruin his fiancé's life. Or drive away from him forever and go on with my pain. Devastated, with the FUCK LIFE attitude, I went home and got drunk, played some slow jams, crawled under the covers and stayed there for two whole days. I missed work and classes not to mention that important exam. I did not answer any phone calls and the only reason I answered the door when Dominique came over was because she kept banging like a damn mad woman. She entered my apartment cursing me out for worrying her like that and I flopped down on the couch still crying. Then she realized I was torn up and her anger turned into concern; what's wrong girl? I couldn't speak; my swollen eyes made her ask did something happen at the party with that dude? Domonique grabbed me and held me like a baby, she let me cry until I was able to tell her what happened. I felt sick and she said baby girl if anybody understands pain it's me. She helped me get showered, made me eat, cleaned my apartment and talked to me until I fell asleep. After about a week; I was able to shake the feeling just enough to get back to my life. I returned to work and school but had a lot of catching up to do. Thankfully my professors were understanding and allowed me to make up my exams and class work. About two months later everything seemed to be getting back to normal except I was feeling a lot of fatigue, with some vomiting and I'd missed one period and was 16 days late for the next one. When I told Domonique she suggested I take a pregnancy test. I told her that I was dealing with some stress and I didn't need to do that. She kept insisting so I did the test to shut her mouth, it came up positive and I couldn't shut my mouth. What in the hell am I going to do? I immediately went to the doctor and he confirmed that I was indeed pregnant between 6-8 weeks and the sonogram also confirmed it was another set of twins. Floored by the news, what was I supposed to do with this information, and what are the odds of me getting pregnant with twins twice? I'm still in school and pregnant by a married man? There was no doubt in my mind that Vincent was the father, just when I thought my life couldn't get any more complicated I was faced with the decision to keep or terminate yet another pregnancy. After some serious soul searching and a river of tears, I decided that to bring children into this situation would be as irresponsible as me having unprotected sex with a man that I knew was getting married just hours after he slept with me. Needless to say I was angry, confused and sad because I was carrying children that belonged to the man that was supposed to be my future husband. I wanted to keep them even if it meant putting them up for adoption but, how could I continue to dance if I was expecting? The bills had to be paid and I had to complete my education or I would really be lost in this strange world. Besides, these children deserved to have both of their parents not just me and it was a struggle to take care of myself. After taking a serious survey of my life I decided to lay on the table and rid myself of these children that did not fit into my school schedule or my future plans of becoming a doctor. This was a complete smack in my face and a sense of selfishness on my part.

Twenty-three years old with no hope for the future if I keep these babies. I took some of my savings and paid for the abortion but this was a difficult decision, yet it had to be done. I scheduled the procedure for the upcoming week because we were on Spring Break, and that would give my body time to heal a bit. However, mentally I was no longer a whole person. I actually wanted to keep my babies because they were the product of real love not a crime like before. Laying on the table, I thought about Vincent and what he would think or feel about me aborting his children. I absolutely hated myself. Domonique was my backbone, she drove me to the clinic and waited to take me back to her house to rest and heal for the remainder of the week. The pain I felt this time was different there was some bleeding that quickly subsided, but my spirit was completely broken. Those fucked up voices in my head kept telling me that some sort of Taboo has to be attached to my life, because everything that I loved either didn't love me back, or belonged to someone else; and the two precious little things that were mine circumstances took them away from me too. As I laid in bed for the entire week my heart felt so hollow but, life has to go on as Domonique says. She was my saving grace and did not allow me to give up on my dream of becoming a successful doctor. Her constant reminders of how losing her first and only love as the result of the betrayal by a supposedly close friend, that resulted in the murder of her husband made me realize that I too could make it. She held my hand through the entire process reminding me that trials don't last always, and that they come to make us stronger. Something my dad preached all the time. Normally that would have pissed me off but for some reason it gave me a sense of comfort that day. She grabbed my hand, looked me straight in my eyes and said, DOCTOR GIRL YOU ARE GOING TO BE ALRIGHT! I made a vow that day to only focus on making money to finish my education and to stay abstinent until I was ready again, if ever. Nothing was going to get in the way of my goals; it was time to really hustle.

The club had become my primary source of income. I was making a substantial amount of tax free money and there was a regular flow of clients. However, Westley was my favorite client who seemed to be interested almost to the point of what appeared to be concern as to why I was dancing in a strip club. I would sit in his lap and we would talk just as much as I danced for him. Trying to have a conversation over the loud music, I explained my situation.

He kept saying you don't belong in a place like this. "What was he telling me that I didn't already know", but how else am I going to pay for my education? He said I will make you a deal. With my eyebrows raised, and my thoughts raced to, Oh Shit! Here we go. He said I will pay for your education, and I said, wait a minute! "What do I have to do for you"? Westley smiled and said calm down lady, all I want is your undivided attention when I am here because I'm not use to having to share anything. I asked is that it? No, if you would accompany me on some business dinners and maybe some out of town ventures. Why me I asked? Because I need a trophy on my arm. A Trophy? Yeah! Silhouette, you must not realize how beautiful you really are, and on top of that your intellect is a turn-on. You Bad Shorty! You have what it takes to boost my morale. I replied, you're funny! But, I heard that you were married. What! Who told you that damn lie? If I were married why would I ask you to accompany me on public outings? Now, I do have female friends, but that won't be a problem because I am not tied to anyone special. OKAY! So what makes me so special that you would request my company in such a personal space in your world? Westley had a way with words, and his response was quite clever. He replied, I'm a businessman; and a smart businessman always seizes the opportunity to invest in a sure fire way of gaining a profit that will allow him to gross more than 100% in ASSets. Bottom line you're a great investment; and you work. More importantly when someone works as hard as you do, it makes since to me to invest in their future endeavors. You hustle hard Shorty, and I've been paying attention. Puzzled, so I asked "Are you sure that's all you want from me"? I don't have to have sex with you do I? Wow! You act like that's a bad thing, but No! It's not a requirement, and I'll leave that up to you. With a smirk on my face, I replied, what do you mean you will leave that up to me? It's just like I said "SIL". "SIL" I chuckled, so wait Westley now you have a pet name for me? He smiled, and said Hold On! By the way what is your real name? I replied, didn't you just tell me you are a smart businessman Westley, so I am sure that you understand the importance of keeping business separate from your personal life. He said, I do! But, I just gave you an invitation into my personal space. I said Okay! You got me, it's Lorraine. Nice name! Real sexy. Thanks Westley, and I agreed to take him up on his offer.

Westley was a perfect gentleman, and our partnership proved to be very lucrative for me. He took me on some very nice trips Miami, New York, Bahamas, and even

Dubai. He spoiled me, everywhere we went, I shopped until my heart was past the point of being content; nice restaurants boasting the finest cuisines, and a personal driver to take us anywhere we needed to go. He damn near paid my entire tuition for medical school. Westley came to the club three or four nights a week when he wasn't traveling. He was a very handsome 46 year old successful, and prosperous investor in the Stock Market, and the CEO of one of the largest Brokerage Firms in New York all while living between two states. Westley was average height about 5'10" medium build, with piercing eyes that sort of told a story that left a hint of mystery about him, and a very sexy smile. The club owner always rolled out the red carpet for him, he sat in the VIP section tailored specifically for him with his rich friends to include some celebrities. Westley put nothing but $20's and $50's on me all night long. So it was a no brainer that when he was at the club he would be my only client on those nights, and it was a requirement that I didn't mind. I'd learned so much working at the Gentlemen's club for the last year in a half. My job was to provide the fantasy for men like Westley, and those whose women refused to supply for their needs at home. It seemed that I was doing my internship because most guys just wanted to talk, to be heard, and have their ego's stroked a bit, while they felt on some Titties and Ass. As I sat in their laps of my clients I also got the opportunity to tell a little bit of my story because most of them expressed the same feelings about my not fitting into that world. However, I had to separate that reality from this reality and keep my focus strictly on why I was there. The music that I danced to, I knew it well and I utilized my hourglass shaped frame to my advantage. As I moved to every beat, lyric, and sound I painted a picture of lasciviousness in their minds. My clients had my full attention, but Westley got special attention. I gazed into his eyes like we were the only two people in the room and made emotional love to him. My dance style is very seductive providing an outpouring of nostalgia that he was missing in another part of his reality. I stood in front of him and moved my body like a snake slithering my way into his deep pockets and his psyche. He watched me with such intensity, and he seemed to be frozen in time. He touched my exposed breast as I raised my arms above my head. He used his hands to sweep my naked body from top to bottom, but not without placing money in the most inconspicuous places. After I finished metaphorically fucking his brains out, I'd always collected close to $1000.00 for the night and I saw him at least three to four

90

times a week. You do the math! But, I would be lying if I pretended that spending all that personal time with him wasn't affecting us personally. Westley was a very nice guy, he treated me like a real woman, and we had some very interesting conversations. We were developing a friendship that would last for a long time. However, this caused some unwanted jealousy between some of the girls and me but this one particular girl Simone also known as "Erotic" who had been dancing at the club long before I came really bitched about it. Erotic had Westley's attention before I came along, then his fantasies shifted in my direction. Domonique "Juicy" always served as sort of road block to keep the haters away from me but, this particular night she wasn't at the club. I went to the dressing room to prepare to go home, Erotic yelled out to me in a snappy ass tone HEY BITCH! I was tired and wasn't for that Bullshit, so I kept it moving. As I proceeded to my car she and two of her sidekicks followed me. I opened the car door, and tossed my bag in the back seat, this chic came up behind me cursing me out. She got up in my face invading my personal space and pushed me, all I could remember was being attacked by my dad and I lost it. This was no cat fight on my end, I was whipping her ass like a prize fighter, and her two friends decided they wanted to jump me. I fought the 3 of them using everything I had until I slipped and fell. One of them said lets fuck her face up and take this Bitch money. I heard that, and thought OH HELL NO! AINT GONNA HAPPEN! I picked up a bottle lying next to me and bust the first bitch in the head that I could get to. That got one of them off of me and the bouncers came running out and snatched the other girl. But, they couldn't help Erotic's ass I'd blacked out and commenced to stumping the shit out of her before they pulled me away. Tony the owner came running out and grabbed me. I was livid and didn't want to be touched he said come back inside and clean yourself up, I refused. First thing I did was get in my car, and pull the sun visor down to look in the mirror to see if my face was messed up because I felt a stinging sensation by my right eye. Dammit! I had a long ass scratch under my eye, two scrapped knees, my hair was out of place, and a missing earring other than that I was straight. When I got home I called Domonique to tell her what happened. She literally hung the phone up on me before I could finish the story and was banging on my door in less than 15 minutes. When she saw me she was pissed, she called Erotic and of course she didn't answer; then she called Tony and told him THEM BITCHES GOTTA GO! He said it's already done.

Domonique said this shit isn't over yet, because those tricks were real disrespectful. I warned them about fucking with you, and they still went at you, but they waited until I wasn't around to do it. I said maybe I shouldn't have took her client. She stopped me and said "Did You Take Him, or Did She Get Sloppy and Give Him Away"? This game ain't about loyalty to them bitches, it's about you getting that paper to survive, before age starts to betray you and nobody want to look at you anymore. We had a few stiff drinks and she smoked weed and I took a puff, it gave me a real mellow high. Mad as hell about my face but after a couple of weeks and some skin cream my scars started to disappear.

Security was heightened at the club after that incident and I always got an escort to my car. Life was hectic and sleep had become a thing of the past; running off of only 6 hours of sleep in 3 days, I went to the club to work for just two hours. Wasn't much happening just a few stragglers and one weird looking guy that I'd given a lap dance, so I headed home to try and get some rest. I decided to walk to my car without a bodyguard when that crazy looking dude came out of the cut on me. Oh shit! I started backing up and he said I'm not going to hurt you, I just want to talk to you. I turned to run back inside and he grabbed me, I screamed as I pepper sprayed his ass. When I got back inside to tell Tony what happened, the guards rushed to the parking lot but he was gone. Paranoid, my stress level was through the roof, and as the world continued to revolve, the evolution started to become too much for me sometimes. I felt like I was being crushed under the weight of life, and the psychological asphyxia was causing my mood to turn Indigo blue. So weed became my new self-inflicted addiction. I smoked before class, between classes, also before and after work. This kept me numb from my reality yet focused enough to not slip in school or in the streets. I'm in my last year of Medical School and started my internship at a local crisis center, but no one had any idea that I was in crisis mode my damn self. This world was different from the world that I'd ran away from so many years ago. However, I'd learned that this world was also a scary place that was no safer than the one I'd left behind. Stuck in the room with nothing but my thoughts, just exhausted! Asking myself, what am I supposed to do? After what seemed like forever I was finally able to fall asleep, and I slept until past noon. I got up, took a shower, dressed, and ate lunch. I had some errands to run, but first I needed to check my mailbox. Rummaging through all of the bills and junk mail I discovered a letter from my childhood best friend Kia. I rushed to open the letter because I had not heard from her in a while. But, this letter wasn't what I expected; shocked Kia was informing me that my dad was dying from brain cancer and that he was asking for me. As much as I hated him for all the pain that he'd caused me, I didn't know what to feel, this was still my dad. But, he hurt me to the core of my being so why should I care? I began wrestling in my mind with the decision of rather or not I should go to see him as he awaits death. Then those childhood thoughts of the good times we had before he violated me caused a tug of war in my head. Fighting with the moral dilemma that was telling me why I should and shouldn't race to his bedside. I was his favorite and he was my best friend at one time. Yet, that time was long gone years ago. Every time I tried to hold on to a good memory of him and there were many, the thought of him raping me repeatedly, stealing my virginity, and impregnating me snatched all of those good thoughts away. The letter said that I should come home right away but that was no longer my home or family just a part of my past. However, studying to be a Psychiatrist had its pros and cons; the student in me said this would be my last opportunity to ask why and try to get some closure, or should I leave him alone to die the way he did me when I was a child. I didn't leave the house for two days, and at the last minute I decided to go and face this man for the last time because this was what I needed. I called Kia to let her know that I was taking a late flight that night, she said make it fast because time was running out.

I arrived at the airport in the early am, and took a cab straight to the hospital. I could smell the stench of death when I entered the ICU and Kia met me at the end of the long hallway that led to the room where my dad was. She hugged me tightly, and I was scared out of my mind, what was I walking into? My entire family was just a few steps away and I had not seen nor heard from any of them in years. We stopped so I could take some deep breaths. The silence was loud and I broke it by saying to myself you are ready to do this. I was finally going to get the closure that I needed when Kia said wait Lorraine, your dad passed 5 minutes ago. WHAT! HE'S GONE! My heart was overwhelmed with grief, anger, guilt, and sadness. Grief because his death also represents the demise of my closure. Anger because that bastard didn't stay long enough to wait for me. Guilt because he was dead and I still harbored hatred towards him, and sadness because I took too long to come. However, this was just the beginning of an interesting reunion that was about to take place. I slid down the wall and curled into a ball on the floor, when I felt someone holding me, telling me that it was going to be okay. But, the voice was one that I had not heard in a very long time; it was my big sister Lena. When I looked up I was surrounded by my family, but they all looked quite different. Lena wore the countenance of melancholy and it appeared that life had beaten her badly. LeAnn was cute or should I say handsome as she stood there looking like a guy with deep dimples that favored my baby sister. Mom had aged drastically, I almost didn't recognize her. I didn't know how to receive them, when mom tried to embrace me I flinched with anger, grief, and disappointment. Hysterical I screamed, PLEASE DON'T TOUCH ME! I needed to see his body to confirm that this was not a dream. My mom was very upset but I couldn't help the fact that I did not want her to touch me. My sisters said we will walk you down to the room; my heart raced and I was physically sick to my stomach. I asked Kia to go with us, she agreed but, the closer I got to the room where his remains rested I started to lose my nerve. What was I going to see, and did I want to see it? It took what felt like a mile long walk to take one final look at my dad, but I froze. A voice in my head said you came this far so there is no turning back now. When I entered the room I looked at my daddy so frail, and what little hair he had left was completely gray. Anxiety kicked in, I hit the floor and began to scream out to the top of my lungs at the sight. For some reason I did not see the man I hated, all I could see was the man that I once adored and now he is gone and never coming back. My mind was in a tail spin, plummeting at a rapid pace and out of control. Why didn't I come sooner so I could have talked to him, I couldn't wrap my mind around his death. I had to be admitted to the hospital and given sedatives to try and calm me. Lena and Kia stayed with me and as soon as I was coherent enough, against doctor's orders I signed myself out. Angry and though this was probably not the most appropriate time to do this but, I felt like being selfish at that point in my life. I went straight to momma's house to talk to her; the anger in my heart caused me to rush inside. Once I was inside my mind slowed quickly when I noticed everything looked the same as it did before I left with the exception that both my sisters were now living at home. I approached my old bedroom, feeling nauseated as pictures flashed in my mind of the many sexual assaults that I'd been exposed to in this room. I slowly pushed the door open and my old room had been turned into a storage space. I thought how symbolic since this room was a place of organized crime that had been stored away in my heart for years. As I toured the rest of the house I noticed that there were new family photos of my sisters with my parents and three very cute little children. But, not even one picture of me in their house anywhere. I don't know why but, that made me sad. What had I ever done to them to be erased from their lives? I had a right to be mad with them they were both abusive hypocrites, and I could suddenly feel the hatred for my parents reappearing in my heart. It's funny although I'd walked out of their lives years ago, rooted somewhere deeply inside my head I expected them to still care about me. They were void of compassion; how they'd lead this crusade of holiness all these years is a great example of how unrestrained conceptualization happens in the church. Heartbroken, I turned to walk out when my baby sister said, "So You Just Going to Leave Again"? Not realizing that she was even in the room, I turned to faced her and said, there's Nothing Here for Me. She replied, "I'm here". I started to weep and she gave me the biggest hug, her embrace was just what I needed. We decided to go for a long walk in the neighborhood that we grew up in. I said to her, things have changed a lot, LeAnn said yeah including me right? Yes, you have, but you're beautiful. My baby sister was a bit on the thick, curvy side, she wore her hair in a long wavy ponytail. Her beautiful bright smile exposed those deep dimples she was born with that played wonderfully off of her hazel eyes, which are no doubt a trait from our mother. LeAnn wore the most expensive clothing by top designers. She took lesbianism to another level, there was a certain amount of finesse that made her look appealing. She is cool and I am proud to call her my little sister. She thanked me for the compliments, then she asked with a look of pain covering her face, what happened sis? Why didn't you ever try to reach out to me or Lena? I paused, at a loss for words. Then she said I know why you didn't speak to mom and dad, but me and Lena never stopped loving or needing you. I said in a somber tone "Nobody needs me". We sat on the stoop of the old recreation center where we never got a chance to play and talked for hours. I learned a lot from my baby sister who was now a lesbian, but the congregation at dad's church had a problem with her personal sexual preference. LeAnn said our parents tried to make her change, as if they had any control over that, and when she refused they kicked her out of our church and the house for a while. Out of curiosity I asked did dad, and before I could complete the question she said Hell No! This girl's personality spit straight fire, she played no games. LeAnn informed me that she knew what had happened to me and Lena but she said I wasn't having it. I asked if what happened to us fueled her decision to becoming a lesbian. LeAnn said my thought has always been if my father, a pastor who teaches the word of God concerning lustful things to a multitude of people could use his own dick to bully, rape, and control his all-female family, then dick must be evil and I wanted no parts of it. Then she said, you make it sound like some sort of morphing process. I didn't become a lesbian I knew I liked girls since I was 7 years old. I SAID, WHAT! She said yeah I had a crush on your girl Kia since I was small, we laughed. Then I asked so what's going on with Lena? She sighed, and said she has been in and out of rehab for the past four years but, she has been clean for almost a year. She was out in them streets prostituting and got pregnant on two separate occasions we don't know who the fathers are but, you have a niece named Ta'Myu, and two handsome little nephews named Sloan and Kai Mecca. They all live with us because mom and dad well I guess now I am raising them; at least until she can get herself completely clean or they grow up whichever comes first. LeAnn insisted that I talk to Lena because she needed my support and she feels like not hearing from you all this time meant that you are disappointed in her. She keeps saying you left because she didn't tell you the whole story, and allowed you to be blindsided by dad's wrath. She explained how Lena went hard in the streets, out of control. She'd been shot, locked up, and for the past few years she would either come home pregnant or to drop off a baby, steal some shit and rollout. But, those kids are the glue that keeps this family together and I can't wait for you to meet them. I explained to LeAnn that I wasn't coming back to stay necessarily, but to face these demons that have been riding my back all these years. But, I promise I will keep in touch with you, Lena, and the kids. LeAnn said what you mean you not going to keep in touch with momma? Okay I do know that mom couldn't talk to you because dad did not want her to, now granted given the situation with dad I didn't like his ass that much myself, but mom has been good to us. That statement really pissed me off! So I asked how much do you know about my situation with mom and dad? Mom was good maybe to you, but Lena and I didn't get that same care. This woman knew her husband our father was raping his daughters, and she threatened that if I ever told anyone I would be punished severely. Does this sound familiar "WHAT GOES ON IN THIS HOUSE STAYS IN THIS HOUSE"? To see Lena who was once a beautiful, intelligent girl that I looked up to, now burnt-out and fighting for her life every single moment she takes a breath pisses me off. Did you know that I was pregnant with dad's kids and they took me to abort them, yes twins and mom seemed to hate me after that. Yet she knew every time he was getting out of her bed to come into mine, but she never spoke a word. The shit they did to their own damn children has caused a "Domino Effect" that not only hurt me and Lena, but is now fucking with your life and the lives of those innocent children. So no disrespect to you, but I don't have shit for your mother right now. Confused LeAnn stood there with her mouth hanging open with surprise, because she'd just learned that her mother was not the angel she thought she was. LeAnn sat back down on the stoop and buried her face into her hands and started apologizing. I assured her that she had no reason to apologize for her parent's sick choices. LeAnn was stuck, her response was, Damn mommy is the sweetest person I know, but now I understand some things a little better. She did allow dad and the church to roast me, and when he put me out she didn't stop him she said nothing. I reiterated that has always been her stance, whatever he said was law. LeAnn said, you have to do what you need to do to move on the best way you can Sis. But, can you do me a favor, would you allow her to bury dad first? In my head I thought "Did she give a fuck when he buried his lust inside of my

103

innocence". However, for my little sister who had just become my personal dump site of secret pain that I never told a soul until now; I felt I owed her that much. We walked back to the house, but I had no desire to go inside. I felt the need to escape the coldness of the 3 D's in that place, Deception, Despair, and Death. LeAnn said I'm going to check on momma and the kids are you ready to meet them? Yeah! I'll be there in a moment. Standing in the front yard when Lena came out and said Hi Sissy. She walked up to me and I embraced her tightly. I could feel pain rushing from her soul as she repetitively said I'm so sorry for leaving you. We cried together, but my tears were because I felt the reconciliation of our sister bond returning and I assured her that I never stopped loving her. As the cleansing process was underway Lena told me that dad started molesting her when she was 9 years old, and mom knew. She further explained that when she was 13 years old she met a 15 year old boy that she liked. They shared their first kiss, but one thing led to another and she had sex with him. Lena continued to explain saying, I only did it because I did not want dad to be my first. But, I knew he eventually would be, and if I was going to avoid that I had to take control of my own body, at least this one time. I told mom that I had sex with the boy and she told dad, he was furious, and about a week later daddy came in my room and raped me while momma sat in the next room ignoring my cries of anguish to her. I endured years of sufferings, and the only thing I knew to do was to rebel in hopes that they would make me leave. When that didn't work I left on my own. Do you remember dad shaved my head? Yeah. I was incredibly humiliated, and that was when the walls started closing in on me, I had to get out. It was either leave or die because killing myself was a thought in my mind almost every day that I was in this house. All those times you asked me why I wouldn't follow the rules I came so close to telling you. But because you and daddy were so close I didn't want to change your view of him. I was hoping that he wouldn't do it to you and I initially thought this was a personal attack on me. I said to her, Lena, it was obvious that something was happening when you left the way that you did. She went on to tell me about her struggles with drugs, prostitution, her children that she loved so much although they were fathered by different strangers. Her lifestyle had taken a serious toll on her body, both mentally and physically. She was so skinny and looked just as old as mom did. I asked her how she did it, how was she able to come back to live in his house after that? She told me that she never really interacted with our parents, and she didn't move back in the house until dad was completely bed ridden. Lena also expressed how grateful she was that they took her babies in. However, she said the thought of him doing something to her children also forced her to come back to their house. She said, Lorraine, all I'm trying to do is stay clean and it's the hardest thing that I've ever had to do. Anything can be a trigger for me, dad's death, a familiar face or hangout spot from my past, the sound of my crying babies when I can't calm them, and even a song on the radio. I have to be very careful of what I allow into my space. To break the ice I said, you have to move over a little bit because I am the space invader and I won't be leaving your side ever again Lena. We both shared a hug and laughed. Then she asked the question "Lorraine would you pray for me", because I know you have a strong relationship with God. Oh Wow! What am I supposed to do, she's crying out for my help and I can't help her with this one. I had to think fast because I refused to pray to a god that allowed my father a pastor to rape and impregnate his own daughter while our mother watched and did nothing. I quickly skipped the subject and told her how strong she was, and if she made it this far, life could only get better for her. She agreed, and we went in the house. As soon as we walked through the door her 3 year old son

Sloan ran, and jumped in her arms with a huge smile on his face. He was the cutest little thing. Lena introduced us, and he gave me the biggest and tightest hug that I'd ever had from a little person, and said Hi Auntie Lorraine; I could feel my heart melting. Ta'Myu and, Kia'Mecca are Lena's 10 month old fraternal twins, and they were the most adorable babies ever. The boy had a head full of hair but the little girl was as bald as could be. Both of them were full of smiles, giggles, and grins, the children's presence helped soften the blow of being in this atmosphere. Meeting my niece and nephews for the first time was sort of bitter sweet. The twins were a painful reminder of the two sets of twins that I'd aborted. Sloan was a breath of fresh air, already charming and quite intelligent for a 3 year old. I played with the children for a while, and as we were getting acquainted in walks momma.

There fell an awkward sort of hush in the room, then momma breaks the silence by saying Hello Lorraine, and I replied Hi Mama. To save face I stood up to greet her; she hugged me for the first time since I was a child and it felt strange. This hug was nothing like the hug that I'd received from Mrs. Coles during my freshman year in college. The longer momma held on to me the more devastated I felt. I pulled back just enough for her to understand but the

107

gesture was faint enough that no one else witnessed the disconnection between us. Lena took the kids and left the room, while LeAnn gave me the look as a reminder about my promise to allow mom to bury dad before we had that inevitable conversation that needed to happen. So here I go again sacrificing my own needs to appease others and I was overwhelmed with everything except peace. Yet, LeAnn remained in the room to ensure her mother's protection. A sense of almost jealousy filled my heart, I definitely did not feel that same need to protect mom as my little sister did. However, I could understand her stance; ever since I could remember LeAnn had been attached to mom's hip. So I consciously inhibited my feelings for that moment. Lena came back to join us and Mom sat down and begin to discuss the details of daddy's funeral arrangements. Both of my sisters and my friend Kia were speaking at his service and she asked if I would say a few words. Staring directly at my sister LeAnn with the look of sinister in my eyes, I quickly turned my focus back to mom and informed her that I wouldn't be able to do that. Did she really just ask me to say anything nice about her husband? It was bad enough that I was here for this shit, and she never offered for me to stay at her house while I was in town but, now she is really pushing it. Mom asked why I couldn't do it, and what are people going to think if your sisters speak and you don't? My response was Hmm! "I See You're Still into the Image Thing" I need to go! Goodnight, and I walked out. The drive back to the hotel was a complete blur, I still cannot remember which route I took to get there. Insomnia set in and I couldn't sleep, I was wrestling with the decision to leave and get back to my life in California or pay my last respect to a man that repeatedly robbed me of my dignity and pride as a young girl. The funeral services were the next day; I intentionally arrived late and sat in the back of the church wearing dark shades hoping that no one would notice me. However, I did notice that my old friend Vincent was there and even he didn't notice me. Unlike, my sisters and many others I refused to get in front of an audience and pretend that my dad deserved the father of the year award. I didn't ride in the family car or go to the grave site with them and that re-past was out of the question. I drove to the grave site and sat in my rental car until everyone left. As the casket sat hovering over the six feet deep hole that would house his body for eternity, I stood in front of it wanting to push it into the hole myself. Instead I sat in the empty chair in front of the corpse in that box and it seemed that my own life was flashing before me. My heart was filled with the pain of the unanswered question WHY? I started to speak to this dead man as if I were going to get an answer from him. I found myself frustrated with the loud sound of silence when I completely lost it, and ended up on the wet muddy ground, groveling in search of relief for the answer. Just when I thought I was alone I could feel someone picking me up from that low place and telling me it was okay. The voice was very familiar it was Vincent. When I looked up his blue eyes gave me some comfort, all I could do was cry but this man took me back to my car and asked if he could drive me back to my mother's house. I said no, but if you could drive me back to my hotel, I just want to be alone. When we reached the hotel he gave me my keys and insisted on walking me safely to my room. I asked how are you going to get home, he said I will catch a cab. I told him that I would drive him, he insisted, No! You are too upset to be behind the wheel of a car. I invited him in the room and grabbed some dry clothes, showered and he waited like a perfect gentleman. I got dressed and came out of the bathroom, he asked if I wanted to talk? I said not right now, then he asked "Can I hold you? I said you're a married man, and he said I'm still your friend and No I'm not married anymore. With a frown of surprise I said it's only been what, two years? He said yes, it seems I have that curse of running women away; so far two for two. I said that's where you're wrong you didn't run me away my dad did. Lorraine what do you mean, because once you left for college you could have reached out. I was tired of the charade and began to cry out of control. He hugged me and asked what's wrong? I replied everything. Pulling myself together I said; I owe you an apology and an explanation for what I'd done to you. But before I explain can I offer you a glass of wine, he said will I need it? I looked him straight in his eyes as he wiped my tears and I said yes. I poured two glasses and started from the night we got caught at the burger spot when we were in high school. There was a lot of shame as I told him what happened that night, even the fact that I was pregnant when we graduated from High school. I told him everything. Vincent was in total disbelief and the tears flowed from his eyes and he apologized and held me so tightly. He said Lorraine why didn't you tell me? I explained I never told anyone including Kia; I just wanted to get away. We talked all night almost like a re-run of our last encounter but, this time was different because a cleansing process was taking place, for both of us. He said I knew something happened but, I would have never guessed that your father would do that to his own child. Your dad was a well-respected man in the community. I said yes he was but, he was nothing short

111

of a monster in our house. I told him that truthfully I only came back to confront my parents but dad died 5 minutes before I got to the hospital, and out of love for my little sister I haven't had that conversation with my mom yet. Needless to say there is still no real closure there. He said okay, now all of this makes sense you pushing me away, the dancing thing by the way are you still dancing. Does it matter? Yes it does. Why? Because I want to help you so you don't have to live that life anymore. Boo there is much that I have had to do to survive that I didn't want to do, but make no mistakes I'm no fool. I know you're not Lorraine. I said Vincent can I ask you a question? Sure, no more secrets, my life is an open book with you. Flattered I smiled; and asked what happened to you and your wife? He sighed, and said where should I begin, the relationship was over before it started Lorraine, after we broke up I did everything I could to fill the hole in my heart. I knew that night we spent together that I shouldn't have married her, not because she was a bad person but because I knew I could never give her all of me because my heart still belonged to you. Before we got married we discussed our future plans, and I wanted three children, she agreed and I later found out that she couldn't conceive. She knew that she couldn't have children, but neglected to tell me that very important detail, we tried everything and spent a lot of money on fertility treatments. One thing led to another and things got worse over time. We put up a great facade in public but at home we barely talked to each other. We tried to hold it together and I'd even considered adoption but she didn't want to do that. One day she left for work and never returned, she told me to find someone that could give me a family. I was devastated and I tried to reconcile our relationship. I told her that I didn't need a baby to seal my love for her but, she still served me with divorce papers, so here I stand all alone again. Vincent told me that he felt guilty for dumping his problems in my lap because it was about me not him. I felt like a jackass, but I had to tell him what I'd done; so I said you aren't the only one in this room that feels a lot of guilt. He replied I understand, and I said No, you really don't. Vincent said do you want to talk about it? I took a deep breath, and said I need to tell you something. I dropped my head and the waterworks began again, the same way he did when we were teenagers he lovingly lifted my chin and asked what is it? Overwhelmed by the reality that I was sitting with Vincent and finally telling him the truth I could barely speak. He said whatever it is baby I have enough love in my heart for you to help you through it. Then I said it, that night we spent together before your wedding when we made love I got pregnant with your children. He said WHAT! I said yes twins and I told him that I'd gotten rid of them. He was extremely quiet as he held me and said don't feel bad I understand why you did it. I told him how it still haunts me today because I really wanted to keep them and looking at Lena's twins made it that much harder for me. After about an hour he said Lorraine, I still love you, even more now than ever before, but I need you to tell me if you love me, Please. YES! Vincent I never stopped but there was a lot of hell raging in my world and I didn't want to pull anyone into my cesspool of life. Curious I asked how he felt about what I'd done; he simply said honestly I am sad about it but happy at the fact that I fathered not just one but two babies with the love of my life. He said I only wish I could have met them, it was at that moment we both agreed that making love right now was appropriate for us. Our session was extremely intense and we did not hold back. Every expression of love was loosed and I allowed my emotions to show. With my legs wrapped tightly around his waist, receiving every stroke of his powerful thrust we rocked pelvis to pelvis for hours until we were both totally satisfied. I allowed myself to confess as I whispered passionately into his ear I LOVE YOU BABY, I could feel sensuality spilling from my soul. We stayed in that room and in each other for two days with no outside contact with the world. Graduation was next week so I told him that I would be leaving in two days, he offered to follow me back to return the rental car. Vincent decided to move back to our hometown Washington DC., after his divorce, so he no longer lived in California. He said I don't live there anymore and until now I had no reason to visit but, if you invite me to your Graduation I would definitely show up. Looking at his reflection through the mirror, with a smile on my face I said, "You're Invited". Vincent reminded me first things first you have some unfinished business with your mom. I Know. He kissed me on the forehead, and replied I'm with you. We showered together, and it was amazing. As the hot water released steam into the atmosphere, the fog was the only thing that could fit in between the dense space that our bodies shared. I turn facing the wall, and Vincent lathered the washcloth with soap and started to wash my back. My hands pressed against the shower wall as if I were being arrested; he bathed me from head to toe, not missing one spot on my body. I gave him the same attention in return. The soap suds made their way down his masculine chest flowing over every rippling muscle on his perfectly formed body.

Standing underneath the hot steamy water sharing a lips locking wet kiss. He disappeared from sight into the hot cloudy mist, but in a split second I not only knew where he was, I felt where he was taking me. Vincent used his tongue to give my pussy a lustful lashing, and when he was done tasting my nectar, while at the same time driving me insane, he picked me up and I wrapped my legs around his waist. His dick slide inside of me with the squeaky roughness of the water that washed us clean, coupled with the slipperiness of the natural secretions that he caused to flow from my vagina that ignited the fire inside of me that was burning out of control. In the midst of a very compassionate kiss we left the shower water running. Vincent stepped out while I was still riding on his stiff apparatus like a see-saw. The cold air made my nipples hard and erect, to the point of an intensifying, euphoric-like pain. He pressed my wet back against the mirror, then gentling laid my naked body on the floor. When he spoke in that melodic voice saying "Lorraine look in the mirror", "Do you like what you see"? It was something about watching Vincent fuck me that turned me on. He was the ultimate, I've never been fucked with that amount of vigor in my life. Bryce was good, but this was another level. When he finished "Blowing my back out' I had carpet

116

burns that I proudly wore like tattoos. This was no fleeting moment, this was the real deal, we were in love and I wanted to go to the next phase in our relationship. After we finished sharing the most magical sexual and mental experience we got back in the shower together, but this time we got dressed. He'd taken the liberty of packing my bags, and asked if I would spend the next couple of days at his house. I said, it looks like you've already decided that for me, so yes I will. We drove to his place first to drop him and my things off. He lived in a very nice brownstone with exposed beams and brick throughout, in a highly sought after neighborhood in uptown Washington, D.C. near restaurants and the night life that is ideal for a young couple. I used his phone to call LeAnn to see if mom was home. She confirmed mom was there, then with an attitude she asked why weren't you at dad's funeral? I was there but sat in the back trying to be inconspicuous. I just didn't feel like being around a bunch of phony ass people who I had not seen since I was a kid. Is Lena there? LeAnn said that's another thing she disappeared during the repast and we haven't heard from her. "Damn" thinking to myself maybe I should have prayed for her when she asked. Are the kids okay, they are fine. I'm leaving for Cali in a couple of days so I'm on my way to talk to mom now. Are you sure that can't wait? NO LeAnn! I've carried this weight far too long and refuse to bear it anymore. LeAnn this is about me not her or anyone else for that matter. I could feel the tension building between us, so I got off the phone and turned to walk out. But, not before Vincent grabbed and reassured me that I was doing the right thing. Then he asked if I wanted him to go with me for support; and I told him that I could handle it. He kissed me, and I was on my way yet, anxiety was taking control. I was about to confront mom concerning her uncaring nature towards me. Fear was getting the best of me and I wanted to turn and run away but, if I wanted to free myself this had to be done. I finally arrived at the house, my heart was racing and I felt almost paralyzed with nervousness. The thought of all that took place inside that house pissed me off all over again. I conjured up the nerves to face this woman that gave birth to me. One might think since she was adopted, her own children being her first and only blood relatives, she would have been more protective. With that in mind, I approached the front stairs and felt a bit more prepared to get this over with. It seemed that with every step I took to get closer to the door, a boldness filled my heart. When I reached the door and turned the knob in an attempt to walk in, it was locked. So I knocked like any other stranger

118

would I guess. The sound of footsteps and the shadow of a woman was apparent through the stained glass door. The knob turned slowly and the door opened, it was Momma. Still standing on the porch because she seemed a bit hesitant about letting me inside; we both looked at each other in complete silence and I'm sure I had the stare of death in my eyes. When she said "Hello Lorraine won't you come inside".